A SCENT OF LILIES

Claire Gallois

A SCENT OF LILIES

TRANSLATED BY
Elizabeth Walter

𝔰𝔇

STEIN AND DAY /*Publishers* /New York

First published in English in 1971
Translation copyright © 1971 by Wm. Collins, Sons & Co., Ltd.
Copyright © 1969 by Editions Buchet /Chastel, Paris
First published in France under the title
Une fille cousue de fil blanc
Library of Congress Catalog Card No. 74-159517
All rights reserved
Printed in the United States of America
Stein and Day /*Publishers*
7 East 48 Street, New York, N.Y. 10017
SBN 8128-1396-0

A SCENT OF LILIES

I BEGAN to love Claire one Sunday in July. Since then, she often comes to my bedside at night. She stands quite still, her arms folded across her chest as if she were cold. When I open my eyes, she is looking at me and I see her tawny hair barring her face. I don't move. I know that one day she won't come back any more. They have told me so, and besides, it's logical.

That Sunday there were six of us at lunch. My father, my mother, Valérie, Olivier, Charles and me. In my parents' house no one has the right to talk at the table before the age of fifteen. Nor to eat french fries or drink wine. Mother was talking about Claire's wedding. Valérie, looking suspicious, was answering her back. She feels there's nothing more to be said about Claire. I should like to love my mother as much as Claire loved her. I have often heard my sisters complain that in their childhood years they knew Mother only from her appearances in their room at night when she came back from a ball (tall and dreamy) in a glittering dress, wearing the pearls and diamonds which my father continues to lock up every night in the strong-box in his study.

Had I known my mother in those days, she would have enchanted me. If you ask my mother for permission to leave the room during a meal she answers smilingly:

'If you really want to go and pee, go on, but you'll get a spanking.'

That Sunday, when the roast was served with french

5

fried potatoes and mashed on one side for us three youngest, I wanted very much to go to the bathroom. The dog began to bark under the table where he was sleeping off his
morning sun. On Sundays the dog is allowed to lie under
the table at mealtimes, other days my mother says he brings
fleas in on the carpet. Outside we heard the crisp sound of
the gravel being crunched by bicycle tires. My father got
up to open the shutters of the french windows. The wind
blew in and we could see the village café-proprietor, out of
breath and scarlet in the face from his ride in the sun. My
father's face suddenly turned red – I see him in a dream with
a table-napkin knotted round his neck – and his voice turned
red too as he demanded what was going on.

I ought to explain that on Sundays the postmistress shuts
up shop. They all rushed to my father's side and I took the
opportunity to slip away to the bathroom at the far end of
the corridor.

It was in there that I heard the laugh. A laugh such as I had
never heard anywhere. As if they had all gone mad. As if
they were sharing a joke whose echo would never cease to
convulse them. I should have liked to laugh too, but you
can't catch up on such a big laugh. It's always like that, you
slip away for a minute and something happens. I ran to
join them, and on going into the dining-room I saw them
bunched together, shaking their heads and biting their
knuckles; they jostled one another and their arms and
shoulders intermingled. Their faces were filled with sunlight. They were weeping.

'What's the matter?' I shouted so that they should hear
me. 'What's going on?'

At last Valérie, that ever-dramatic beanpole, turned round.
She said, in the tone she would have used to needle me:

6

'Claire's had an accident.'

On the walls which had grown dark the light began to spin, a dizzy solar wheel which thinned out as it whirled. In three seconds it had become as pure as a diamond set down in the sun and I knew that Claire was dead.

I had prayed so hard to stop being a child. My mother let go of my father, she raised her face to heaven, she said in a new voice:

'Above all, I want my child to have extreme unction.'

She adores extreme unction. She has received it five times, each time one of us was born, and she very nearly had it administered to Charles last year when Olivier threw his Indian knife at him and caught him in the throat. Charles has a baby's face, without features or memories. At six, he still wears rompers. He is not very clean and not very independent in this respect and my mother thinks it's easier to unbutton between his legs or even to leave it open – it hardly shows – than to undo trousers and braces. I remember Charles last year coming back to the house on his wobbly little legs, holding his chin with both hands, and I remember the timid, bewildered air that his wound gave him. For Claire's accident he was crouched almost under the table and he was gazing into the void with the same expression of surprise.

I crouched down beside him. I took him in my arms, and we watched the others milling about and suffering. Charles always smells of brioche. When he had been reassured a bit, I whispered in his ear:

'Claire's going to die, darling.'

He nodded his head energetically. Olivier was clutching Mother's waist, he was butting his head against her stomach and yelling for her as if he was lost in the dark. Mother picked him up in her arms, she covered him with kisses. Later on, everyone said:

'Without Olivier, Véronique would have gone out of her mind.'

Véronique is Mother. She never punishes Olivier, not even when you tell on him.

Outside the sun went on shining. It no longer mattered about keeping the house cool. Shutters clattered, doors banged. Papa's face got redder and redder, every five minutes he put his hand to his cheek and then looked at it as if he expected to find it stained. Charles and I burrowed further under the table. On the floor above we heard Mother walking about very fast and firmly and calling out instructions to Valérie. She was busy collecting black clothes in case Claire died. Her footsteps moved towards the old nursery which serves as a linen closet and hanging cupboard now that we are older. I like this room with the little bath in which now you have to tuck your legs under you to get them covered with water, and the wallpaper with the miller, his son and the donkey which we had each in turn torn and peeled back on moonlit evenings when it was boring to go to sleep. On my wall I had scratched 'Red Nose' with a compass point. That's what I call my sister Valérie when I am in a rage. Her nose has been remodelled. Against a bright light it is like an unpolished glass. I made a resolution, if Claire really died, not to call Valérie 'Red Nose' any more and not to quarrel any more with anybody. Valérie came into the dining-room in search of a glass of liver salts. She often has bilious attacks. Her mouth and nose were going white. A big pale ring. When she saw Charles and me under the table, she thought better of it and said:

'I don't care if I *am* ill when Claire is suffering.'

After a moment she added: 'You know –' and her lips trembled, her eyes turned up, and I thought she was going to disappear – 'you know, I'm offering God my life in exchange for Claire's.'

I could scarcely breathe. Despite myself, I cried out:

'Let her die. Can't a person even die peacefully round here?'

My mother came running. She put her arms round us, her eyes were pale, she repeated:

'Lord, Lord, keep my little girl alive. Even if she's crippled, paralysed, disfigured, keep Claire alive for me.'

She got up, and in her look one part of her past was destroyed for ever. She said again:

'They're hiding the truth from me.'

And after that, she forgot all about us.

My father is mad on photography. He owns an old folding Kodak which gives very clear pictures in which we are always more beautiful than normal, no doubt because he has misjudged the distances, or rather, because he has focused on infinity once and for all. When we were all ready – my younger brothers in last winter's brown trousers with braces; my mother in her hat which she keeps for weddings, her face a water-colour under the different layers of pink which she puts on mechanically, harmoniously; Valérie in a white piqué dress, with black patent heels, and powdered up to the eyes to sop up the tears – when we were all ready he lined us up once more on the steps of the terrace.

Every summer he takes the same picture all over again, just as he checks the pencil marks on the bathroom door to see if we've grown. Charles 3 ft. 6 ins., Olivier 4 ft. 8 ins., me 5 ft. 2 ins., Claire 5 ft. 3½ ins., Valérie 5 ft. 7 ins. We shall never touch them again. He wanted to leave a step vacant between Valérie and me: Claire's step. In this photograph we all have our heads down. My mother entreated:

'Jérôme, Jérôme, hurry up. I want to see her alive.'

My father had not changed. He was wearing the same suit he had worn at lunch, a grey suit which now seemed too light. He didn't appear to have heard. His knuckles whitened on the camera. The shutter clicked, and he collapsed into a chaise-longue, his head turned to one side. He said he wouldn't budge. Cars were instruments of death. He would never touch his again. Or else he would buy a tank to crush all the cars that had crushed Claire. Charles looked wide-eyed at Papa, despite the heat his teeth began to chatter. My mother let her arms fall, she seemed shrunken all at once. She kissed Papa on the cheek, like a child. She said to him:

'Suppose you lie down a bit? You could join us later, when you feel better. I haven't the courage to wait for you.'

To me she said very quietly:

'Stay with your father. See that he doesn't do anything silly.'

She left the suitcases with me too, and she and the other three set off for the station on foot.

Papa made up his mind at last. He and I left all by ourselves in the big Peugeot made specially for us with the two little pull-down seats between the big ones because as a rule we were five children, plus two parents, plus Henriette, plus a grandmother sometimes. The heat spread over Papa. He twitched, he closed his eyes, his head drooped and then came up again. Usually, when there is no gendarme in sight and I am alone with Papa, I hold the steering-wheel over his hands. Papa was more or less numb with tears. He had shiny tracks on his cheeks, like those left by snails. I had never seen Papa cry. I kept telling myself that Claire was dead, or that she was going to die, and it didn't mean a thing.

We drove on, passing people drinking orangeade or gathering flowers in the ditches. On thinking about it, I should have preferred us to experience an earthquake or a fire; something real, at any rate. Sometimes Papa put his hand on mine for a second, and I withdrew it. In a choking voice he began to say all over again that he wanted to bash all the cars, crash into the murderer who had crashed into Claire. He swerved too sharply in front of a six-wheeler with a trailer. I saw the double wheels almost as high as the roof of the car, and then Papa sank down yet again into the depths of his seat, he put his hands over his face, the driver of the six-wheeler was blaring, blaring on his horn, I saw his face glowing red behind the windshield, and I knew that the great wheels scented us, the great wheels were going to crush us. I waited for death and Papa exploded with rage. We drank Coca-Cola at a service station, but Papa made a move to show the attendant the telegram about Claire, and I pulled him back by the sleeve. For the rest of the journey we didn't say another word.

We came to a big open space, a sort of cross-roads where the highway came out, with a café or restaurant on one side with a terrace and flowers. Opposite the café there was a police car with a radio mast and a gendarme diverting the traffic. Around the car there was a crowd of people with their backs to us. Papa parked the car in front of the café and we got out. We held hands tightly, and the crowd parted, and we were out of breath and then we saw behind the crowd a gendarme with a steel inchtape taking measurements on the ground.

He straightened up, putting his hands to his back. At the edge of the asphalt, near a seat in the shade of some plane-trees, they had drawn a chalk silhouette stretched out, arms flung wide, one leg short and the other long, and blood, blood everywhere, in spots and streams right into the gutter, blood so thick in places that the chalk mark hollowed out pink channels. The air was full of glittering splinters, you had to blink your eyes and it was sickeningly hot. Papa let go my hand, everyone was looking at us, and they went on staring at us even when we shut our eyes. The good lady from the café wanted to make me go away and pushed at my shoulders, she wore a yellow dress and too much lipstick. What could this poor fool know about this blood, it wasn't her blood. I put on Mother's voice:

'You might have thrown a bucket of water over the road when you knew the relatives were going to come.'

Papa turned round. The gendarmes had a mourning air. I had a wild desire to bark. I took Papa's hand again and we listened to the explanations. At the time I didn't remember any of it, but since then I've learnt it all by heart because right up to the trial Papa never stopped going over the details. At the end I tugged at Papa's sleeve:

'Is she still alive?'

'Yes, yes,' Papa said, distressed and preoccupied.

And dogs began to jump about in the sunshine, the cars had butterfly-nets sticking out of their windows, and the people on the terrace tinkled the ice afresh in their glasses of lemonade. We hurried to get back in the car.

On top of a hill, as far as I remember, there was a maternity clinic run by nuns. I don't know why Claire was taken there. A young nun with dimples greeted us on the steps. She gently urged us to cry very quietly so as not to upset the mothers who had just had babies. She skipped lightly along the white corridor, making the folds of her habit flutter. She told us that all her sisters were praying for us and that our dear Claire undoubtedly had her place among the angels. She pushed open the door of the room with unheard-of precautions, opening it half way first, poking her winged headdress round, then proudly withdrawing to allow us to enter.

It was almost dark around Claire's bed. I wondered if the nun had remained outside the door to make sure we weren't going to cry too loudly. After a few seconds we could make out some lilies in a jam-jar on the bedside table. I heard Papa's breathing. In this room everything was peaceful. Claire was lying on her back, her hands clasped. She wasn't like she used to be. She seemed much older.

It isn't really Claire. From under the mass of bandages swathing her head like a nun's headdress, several strands of tawny hair stick out, grown stiff and almost russet. Her nose seems tiny, probably because her cheeks and chin have swollen. Her mouth is half open and her teeth are showing as if in a smile. Icy, bluish teeth.

Papa said he was glad Mother hadn't seen all that. Papa is always a bit behind. I think he was speaking of Claire outlined on the road. He brought out his old folding Kodak and rested it on the bed-rail while he counted one, two,

three, four, five for the exposure. All the people who
have seen this photograph have congratulated Papa on
Claire.

It's true, Claire is smiling in death. I only hope her lips
have been drawn back by the powerful muscles contracted
by the blow which broke her neck. In this photograph
Claire is a vessel void of darkness and of light.

After the photographic session, Papa pulled the only chair
in the room up close to Claire and sat down on it. He made
as if to take her hand and drew back quickly, as though he
had allowed himself a crazy gesture. He looked at me re-
proachfully, and as I was blushing redder and redder, he
said slowly:

'Go on, dear, kiss your sister.'

When I'm scared, I am incapable of disobeying. I con-
sidered with the utmost care where I could kiss Claire
without causing Papa distress. Not on her swollen cheeks.
Not on her temple, where the mass of bandages left in-
sufficient room. On her forehead. Where something living
remains inscribed on marble statues.

For minutes and minutes afterwards I continued to feel
scared. Suppose you went on indefinitely having a mouth so
dry you could never spit again.

Mother arrived with Valérie. She had made a détour to
leave Olivier and Charles with Henriette. Henriette has
looked after all of us when we were babies, Mother and
Aunt Rebecca included, but not Papa and Grandma.
Mother flung herself on Papa as if he were her new child,
they stood locked in an embrace, they reached out for
caresses as caresses must be awaited in the last desert, they
inhaled the tears on each other's faces, they withdrew to

arm's length and all the drama and loneliness in their eyes
melted and they leaned close and confidential over Claire;
they bent over her as if over a cradle, and Mother even
smiled. Our tears rained down, our arms, shoulders, fore-
heads mingled, and I even loved my sister Valérie. Claire
was among us, sweet, smelling of ether, we moved her
accidentally and the nun said sternly:

'Don't touch the dead girl, please.'

We all drew back quickly. Mother was the last to straighten
up. She said gently, tenderly:

'She's still so supple . . .'

Then she opened her eyes very wide and added:

'Go out, all of you. I want to see my child naked one
last time.'

I am constantly ashamed of my parents. I have always
dreamed of being a unit set down on the earth, without
origin. Mother is very embarrassing. She doesn't wear a
bra or a girdle, nor have pins in her hair. She says she hates
restrictions. She makes a noise in the bathroom when she
gets up in the night. If she happens to punish us, afterwards
she comes to ask our forgiveness. You don't know where to
look. There she is in front of us, and her eyes become ever
more hot and blue, she says:

'My poor darling, you have a hopeless mother, a nervy
mother, a mother who doesn't really love you one bit.'

And she laughs. We just sigh. Often, she isn't even dressed
for lunch. She wanders around in something lacy and low-
necked. At table she announces that she isn't hungry, she has
to slim. Or else she invents diets, for three days she eats only
figs, or boiled rice, or Gruyère, and she gets upset over
nothing. Papa grumbles that he would rather have her put

on a bit of weight and be better-tempered. Then Mother tosses her napkin aside, she goes off and shuts herself in her room. Five minutes later she is heard crying. I am certain she cries near the keyhole. Papa puts on a harassed air, he orders one of us, without much conviction, to go and console Mother. Claire is always willing. Claire loves Mother to distraction. I have seen her endure swipes with a wet duster without flinching, without batting an eyelid, without a murmur. It is Mother who begins to sob that Claire is killing her. Claire is the only one whose forgiveness Mother never asks.

Valérie and I waited, our hands crossed behind our backs, leaning against the corridor wall outside the door of the room where Claire was lying. We dared not talk of it, but we knew quite well – and so did Mother – that if Claire had been alive she would not have wanted to be laid out naked and stared at. The nuns never stopped fluttering past us. There wasn't one of them who could turn the corner without a fold of her habit dusting the radiator. They made cheering, comforting signs to us. And then it was time for the pots of flowers.

Dozens of men arrived almost simultaneously with flowers. They weren't for Claire, not yet. They opened the doors one after the other, as in a game of follow-my-leader, and each time this corridor was flooded with bursts of sunlight, wailing of infants, and tender twitterings. Everyone was calling everyone else 'darling' in there.

At last Claire's door opened. The blind was now half up. Mother had points of light in her eyes, as if she had just made a discovery. Claire's complexion was blotchy.

'Isn't it stupid,' Mother said, 'she has a pimple on her

forehead and I thought we ought to put some calomel on it.'

Mother and Father looked proud of being so much at ease with Claire. Father had resorted to his old nervous habit of picking his nails and knitting his brows all the time. Mother kissed Valérie and me. She swore to us that she would never punish us again. Then we had to swear to her that we would never ride a bicycle again. Claire had been killed on a bicycle. So when we are in the country we're going to be absolutely tied.

'Nor Olivier and Charles?' I asked her.

'No one,' she said. 'Ever again. Oh God! Oh Claire!'

Since then my mother has been afraid of bicycles. In the car, if she sees a cyclist on the side of the road, she cries out and grabs Papa's steering-wheel.

The nun slipped in once again without shutting the door properly, she had her head on one side. Mother respects nuns, she says they've got me taped. Naturally, though, at boarding-school I don't argue about orders, there's only one thing that interest me and that's growing up.

The nun came and whispered close to my mother and my mother rose with a cry, she begged them not to put her daughter in the mortuary. She clung to Papa:

'Jérôme, do something.'

Papa said you couldn't do anything on a Sunday. He cleared his throat and the nun said, fingering her rosary, that her mortuary was completely private, only babies and a young woman of Claire's own age, nineteen. Mother didn't want to listen, she didn't want to leave Claire, she wanted to keep her all to herself, night and day, until they buried her.

'But,' the nun pointed out, 'after tomorrow you'll hit the Fourteenth of July, which brings us to Thursday at the

earliest, and that makes us a bit late. Not to mention the
room; it's booked, you see . . .'

A room had been booked at the Crillon for Alain and
Claire on their wedding night. Mother offered the nun a
donation for her charitable work. At that moment my ex-
future brother-in-law entered, and everyone fell silent.

Alain always smiled sweetly at Claire. We had never seen
him suspicious or angry. Mother claims you never really
know a man until he says 'Shit!' in front of you. Whenever
Mother says it, the word is just plain embarrassing. You can
hear she has to force herself to say it, and she always em-
barrasses me when she does things like that. Once she took
Olivier and me aside for a talk about sex. Olivier nearly
died laughing and wanted her to draw some diagrams. I
told my mother to buy me a book on the subject and we
never mentioned it again. I can't stand people telling me
what's going to happen to my body. One evening Claire
came out of Mother's room crying. 'All right, the harm's
done now, I haven't got your blasted virginity any longer,'
she sobbed, as only Claire could sob, or laugh, or walk
along the ridgepole of our house in the country with her
arms spread wide like wings, or imitate an owl's cry by
blowing through her clasped hands. I know Mother is
going to remember all this. She will feel awful.

It is only quite recently that Mother began being nice to
Claire. At Easter, when Claire blossomed into beauty. It was
as if a great ray of light had shot through her. Everything
about her – teeth, hair, eyes, skin – suddenly began to glow.
Everyone, people in the street and everywhere, would look
at her and smile. Valérie never stopped trying to explain
away Claire's new beauty. She shrugged her shoulders:

'It's a special look she puts on to attract the boys.'

I don't mind Valérie too much, as a rule. I'm the only one who dares to slap her. Because I'm not tall enough I wait until she's sitting down, or else I climb on a chair when she's forgotten all about our row. When I feel really mean I tell her that some day I'm going to get up in the middle of the night and sock her on her remodelled nose. Every time I'm horrid like that I hate and despise myself, but I know the only way for me to become really good is to wait and grow up. Mother didn't notice at first that Claire had become beautiful. She went on getting worked up; she used to put her hand to head, just like Grandma does, and say:

'Claire, you're wearing me out.'

Claire would break off in the midst of a shriek of laughter and give Mother an expectant, rather sad look. Mother would turn her back or go out of the room, her causes for complaint having vanished in the same instant as Claire's laughter. It was at Easter, too, that Alain appeared on the scene. He looked at Claire and Claire went quiet. Mother made quite a thing of it. At long last she bought Claire some new clothes. Up to then she had shortened Valérie's old dresses for her. Claire was not sent back to Switzerland, or England, or Germany, or wherever Mother can find a family who will keep her shut up in the evenings. Now she wore white wool slacks and a hacking jacket edged with brown for lunch at the Polo Club at Bagatelle, an emerald-green tunic for dinner at Maxim's, a whirl of wild silk to go dancing with Alain. Mother used to get irritable during the fittings and say to the dressmaker:

'Don't emphasize her bust like that!'

'I'm not emphasizing it, madam, it's there.'

The dressmaker mumbled with her mouth full of pins.

19

Claire blushed a bit, but her eyes were laughing slyly. Alain
had asked Mother for her hand. Mother, not my father.
Papa makes a joke of things, so in this family everything is
kept from him. Alain had spent two years as a Trappist
monk. Mother doesn't want us to say anything about it so
as not to disparage him. Papa says the idiot (Alain) has missed
his chance of getting into his father's bank and that his
brother (less of a fool) has benefited instead.

Mother retorts that he still has the income from his
mother's fortune and he can always catch up on the bank
later when his father dies. Alain said he fell in love with
Valérie, Claire, and even me, all at once. He chose Claire
because she is the liveliest. At Claire's engagement party
Valérie went and hid in the kitchen to cry. Mother received
the congratulations with a discreet smile; Alain was everything Claire needed, he would know how to break her in.
Mother often speaks of Claire as if she were a wild young
horse with a tawny mane. Papa never stopped downing
champagne. He slapped his fellow-members of the Légion
d'Honneur on the back and said:

'One up and two to go now, old man. You don't happen
to have a son the right age?'

Mother kicked him, and Papa went 'Ouch!' and hopped
about like they do in funny films. Henriette said that Claire's
diamond was worth at least twenty-five thousand francs.

Claire's hand seemed to get smaller and smaller, she kept
hiding it behind her back. I think Claire found this Alain
business pretty complicated. She no longer laughed when
she looked at him. She used to come up slowly, take his
hand in both hers, and rub her nose and forehead against his
shoulder, the way a young horse rubs up against the trunk
of an apple-tree.

When Alain appeared at the door of Claire's room in the clinic, he was carrying a huge sheaf of flowers for her. He came in without looking at anyone, marched straight up to her and deposited the flowers on her legs. Now she looked deader than ever. Alain's lips were quivering. He took Mother in his arms and she shook her head a few times and shut her eyes. He called her 'Mother'. Then he clapped Papa on the shoulder and called him 'Father'. The nun had crossed her hands on her stomach. She was marvelling at us.

We stood round Claire's bed for ages, gazing at her so hard she almost stirred. The scent of the lilies had a drowsy sweetness. I cast Claire's name into space, upon the waves of silence, as if I had Papa's dog-whistle. You blow it and you can't hear anything, but Bobby hears it miles away and comes running. A dozen times I did it. Claire ... oh, CLAIRE! I thought of Claire on her bike, her hair streaming behind her. She was laughing and the sun was on her laughter. I thought of that car coming and Claire going flying over its bonnet. I thought of Claire crying out, crying out and then ceasing to cry. Had she cried out?

I found the nun at the far end of the corridor. She was folding compresses on a metal trolley.

'What has been done to my sister?'

She looked up for an instant and her glasses caught the light.

'Nothing much. She was dead on arrival.'

'Then what are all those bandages round her head for?'

She replied, like Little Red Ridinghood's grandmother:

'To hide her injuries, my child.'

Were there other injuries hidden by the sheet? The nun said, as if it was a mere trifle:

21

'A compound fracture of the leg and the femoral artery's severed.'

'Did she cry out?'

'What do you think! She never had time.'

In any case, Claire had not been at fault. The gendarme had told Papa she had the right of way.

I hardly knew Claire. All during these years I was at boarding-school. When I came home, I slept in her room. She did not want to waken me. She got dressed with the shutters still closed. She put on a tee-shirt and blue jeans, she brushed her hair for a long time, she had thrown her head back and it flowed down to the ground with a crackle of electricity. She spent an hour on her make-up, she was smiling and humming like someone whom things are going to happen to, and then she came across to my bed.

'Listen, you, don't pretend to be asleep. Tell Papa I've chosen the shell design for the silver spoons.'

That was all. She didn't say goodbye or anything. She went away and she is dead. She rejected us all. She fooled us all. She can jolly well wait for me to cry over her. Claire has lost a face. She has lost her features as one loses a magic formula. I should like to be this stranger.

Alain took us back to Paris. Mother stayed at Claire's side with Papa. Our eyes were half shut against the wind. The sun had not yet set. Alain had put the top down. He was smoking as he drove, he let his left hand dangle outside, and we cruised slowly as we do on holiday. Valérie sat next to Alain, in Claire's place.

Alain stopped to buy us ices at a kiosk with gilded balls fixed to the roof. We ate them solemnly by the roadside,

licking them with the tips of our tongues. The passing cars
flattened our skirts against our legs. I repeated to myself
three times: Claire will never again eat strawberry ice-
cream cones. And afterwards?

'And afterwards . . . nothing. And afterwards, it's so
long . . .'

Claire says that sometimes in the night when she thinks
I'm asleep, and she talks of other things too, and she cries
very quietly and laughs very loudly, and I'm afraid she'll
realize I'm awake.

In the flat in Paris the furniture was covered with dust
sheets, the ashtrays were empty, the vases unfilled, the
carpets rolled up. The doors were swinging open. In the
hall Claire had forgotten her raincoat, thrown over a chair.
Valérie took it in passing, quite naturally, crossed the inner
hall which leads to our rooms by way of a wall of sliding
mirrors, and there – she was in shadow but I saw her – she
slipped into Claire's new raincoat and turned in all directions to see if it suited her. I crept up on her without making
a sound and said sweetly:

'Are you helping yourself to it?'

She looked at me in the glass and said:

'I'm reserving it, anyway. There's no reason why someone else should have it.'

We looked at each other until the reflection blurred.

'What's the matter with you? What is it you want?'
Valérie asked.

I didn't do it on purpose. I said stupidly:

'I want Claire to keep her raincoat.'

I loathe Valérie's remodelled nose. I loathe her smell
which no one else notices. I loathe the fact that she takes
laxatives. I loathe her at Christmas. At Christmas Claire

gives you a paperknife of elder-wood on which she has carved three nightingales with the point of a penknife. She said they were nightingales.

Henriette bustled up holding Charles in her arms wrapped in a bathrobe. Her face was damp and swollen like a sponge. She had taken off her apron and her black dress made her look as if she was in mourning; she said to us:

'A calamity like that, it isn't possible, such a lovely girl, the pick of the bunch, I'm losing my wits, that's three baths I've given your brothers and they haven't so much as murmured, poor drowned rats.'

Behind Henriette's back Valérie looked at Alain and tapped her forehead. Henriette opened the drawing-room shutters and brought in a big jug of cold punch with floating slices of oranges and lemons. All the ice-cubes tinkled. She said it was still necessary to receive Alain correctly, the poor man, a widower before he was even a husband. Alain brought out a notebook from his pocket and ticked off names on a list with a gold pencil. Then he took the telephone on to his lap. Valérie held out to him a frosted-up glass with a rim of sugar. He put his hand on the back of Valérie's neck as she sat beside him and, clamping the telephone receiver between his ear and his shoulder, he dialled with his free hand. He sipped his drink and informed people that Claire was dead. Yes, killed instantly. She had not suffered. Her face was unmarked, thank God.

Grandmother Cartet came to dinner with us. She has the keys of the flat attached to her own bunch and you can hear her jangling a long way off. She was dressed in black, smelt of Coty's Emeraude, and spoke so low you had to be quiet to hear her; beneath her bowed shoulders her

breath came gaspingly. Pearls flowed among the silken folds
of her dress and her fingers got caught in them. She had
bought a chicken in aspic and a pineapple tart. She ordered
Henriette to get Olivier and Charles up so that we could all
pray together. She kissed us so mournfully that it sent a
shiver down our spines.

She kissed Alain too, pulling him towards her by his tie.
It is Grandma's special gift to make us revert to being
children. As soon as she appears we have to stand up and
break off whatever we are doing to give her our undivided
attention. She says, half jokingly:

'Who knows how much longer you're going to see me
around? At my age you weigh no more than a feather, a
puff of wind, and pouf! Granny's gone.'

She must have been really upset over Claire. She took
Alain's arm to go into the dining-room. She looked at the
big bay-window over her sky-blue glasses and recalled the
day – was it only yesterday? – when we had fought so
violently that the cream cheeses for dessert shot across the
table and flattened themselves against the glass. Adjusting
her gaze, she said:

'But deep down you love one another very much, don't
you, darlings? You must love one another even more at
present if you are not to feel the pangs of remorse.'

She sighed, and sighed again.

'Your poor mother, did she ask for me often?'

We said, 'Yes, Granny, but she doesn't want you to tire
yourself out over there.'

She buried her nose in her handkerchief and said through
it:

'Why does my old life have to be spared?'

We didn't know what to reply. The dining-room was

filled with the scent and colour of a summer evening. As if our words and gestures weren't real, as if Claire hadn't died. Pineapple tart is my favourite dessert.

As a rule, three bronze cupids in the middle of the table bear on their wings a basket filled with camellias or black grapes. Mother's rings sparkle when she toys with her transparent knife-rest. The cut-glass stoppers of the decanters refract the wine's pale or dusky light. Our chairs have deer-feet with genuine cloven hooves; unfortunately Olivier, Charles and I have torn the leather seats. The saffron curtains make believe that there is always sunlight. When Henriette hands round the plates you can smell the warmth of her underarms, and her dress gives a bit at the armholes. Against the light from the bay-window Claire's hair is astonishingly pale. She puts her elbows on the table and winks at Charles, who laughs and plops the back of his spoon into his mashed potato. Mother taps Claire's elbow with the handle of her knife.

'Did you do that on purpose?'

If Claire says yes, there's a scene. There is a scene every mealtime. Olivier insists on having a mug for his milk like American soldiers drink out of. He made Mother run the clippers over his head and he lurks in the corridor with a machine-gun to fire rubber darts at our legs. I annoy him by telling him that with his skinny legs and his close-cropped head he looks like a German civilian in the ruins of Berlin. At table I manage to drink his milk at a gulp. He yells and Mother's nerves snap, it's always more peaceful when I am at boarding-school. There are tears pricking behind my eyes but I smile at her, I smile in her face and she shouts.

'Stop looking at me like that. Jérôme, do something!'

Papa is so fed up that he gets up and announces he's going to the cinema. He slams the front door, but as he will come back ten minutes later, we aren't worried. While he's away, Mother cries. She says that she and Papa were so happy before we were born, and before we tore the leather chair-seats.

Tonight, however, no one squabbled. My grandmother picked the carcase of the chicken with skilful fingers. She calls the pope's nose 'a certain part'. Alain inadvertently poured me some wine and I drank it. Valérie helped Alain reckon up on his fingers the details they must start attending to tomorrow. Cancel the wedding invitations. Send back wedding presents to those people Claire hadn't yet thanked. Share out the expenses which Papa and Alain had undertaken jointly in connection with the new flat for after the wedding.

Valérie raised moist eyes.

'And you're going to live there all alone, Alain? It's too sad.'

Alain suggested that we should use the familiar '*tu*' when speaking to him. He looked at us calmly, sensibly.

When he got married in December, Henriette said belligerently:

'I could see that one wasn't exactly broken-hearted.'

But monastic types are like that, for them death is just another Mass. At boarding-school, when one of the nuns dies, we have chocolate cream.

My grandmother's head was a bit heavy, she rested her forehead on her hands and talked of all the dead who had grown up around her: Aunt Clémence, who at eighty could still do high kicks over a chair; her brother, young Jean-Louis, who dropped dead after lunch forty years ago; her old friend Clotilde, and a great many other people whom we didn't know. She forgot Grandfather, but we didn't remind her about him.

Claire was growing more and more distant. I was afraid someone might speak her name. I was afraid she might come back. I remembered the scent of the lilies in the clinic; I got down from the table, and that day was so extraordinary that no one said anything. I didn't want to sleep in Claire's room any more.

I was in a room which we call 'Napoleon' because Papa has made it into a proper memorial to the Emperor, with a glass-fronted cabinet, kept locked, in which are his hat, the pistols with mother-of-pearl handles belonging to the King of Rome, the cavalry swords of three or four marshals like Ney and La Bédoyère, and the trumpets and standards of their regiments. The whole room is full of golden bees – on the walls, the curtains, and even on the bed, which comes from Malmaison. You can get so bored at Malmaison on Sundays!

I lay down with the sheet over my head and pressed my fists into my eyes to see the red stars go past, I usually adore that. But I began to think of Claire, her eyelids not properly closed, her hands clasped in a funny way, her skin cold when I had to kiss her.

Sometimes, at our house in the country, Claire takes me out at night under the trees. Beyond the bend in the path the light from the windows vanishes and it is so dark that we have to hold hands so as not to lose each other. Without warning Claire lets go of my hand, and immediately I don't know if she is near or far. She joins her palms together like a conch shell and blows into them, first it is an owl or a siren in the fog, then it becomes a wail as if someone was unhappy in the darkness, and suddenly I feel Claire's hands on my face like a soul issuing from the ground.

I started to scream. I screamed so loudly that the threads binding me to 'Napoleon' were broken and I set off for the horizon; the years cracked one by one behind me and I was free, caught up by those bodies which complete their revolutions around the sun during the nights of August, and we below say, 'Look, a shooting star.'

I woke up with a start. Valérie was shaking me.

'Are you ill?'

I said: 'I saw Claire at the foot of my bed.'

I ended by communicating my fear to Valérie. She brought her mattress into 'Napoleon'. From time to time we asked each other 'Are you asleep?' so that we didn't drop off. This gave us the feeling that we were defending ourselves against Claire and that she wouldn't be able to get at us. Two cars came roaring into our street, they braked under our windows and we heard the slamming of doors and people laughing. I got up and leaned over the balcony. I saw two ladies in long dresses as if straight out of a magazine and two men in dinner-jackets, it was just such a scene as I picture myself in later on and which gives me the patience to grow up; it made me really mad and I called out:

'Can't you be a bit quiet? There's someone dead up here.'

There was a silence. The cars drove off quietly. After a moment Valérie said:

'You do exaggerate, really.'

Papa flung open the door of 'Napoleon'. He saw us squeezed

on to the same mattress, in the end we had gone to sleep together, and he said:

'My poor darlings, you *have* been left alone.'

He strode across to the window, opened the blinds, and the sun made us curl up under the sheets. In the street a watering-cart gave off a scent of rain. Papa was in shirt-sleeves, he looked like a screen prisoner with his collar undone and his cheeks unshaven.

Papa doesn't like us getting up late; he comes into our rooms holding his thumb to his lips to imitate the mouthpiece of a bugle and sounds the alarm.

'Fall out there! Boche skirmishers coming!'

You get up, startled, and by the time you realize it's a joke it's too late to nod off again, sleep has gone for good.

But today Papa's haste was different, as if he had received a fresh telegram; we sat up wrapped in the sheets and rubbing our eyes, and Valérie grumbled:

'It's barely six, Papa.'

'Fall out!'

'But what exactly is the matter?' Valérie protested. 'First of all, go out so that we can get dressed.'

At that moment Charles appeared; he was holding the paw of his Teddy-bear Céleste who was trailing on the ground. He hung on to Papa's leg and repeated after Valérie:

'What's the matter, Papa? What's the matter?'

Papa shook Charles to make him let go of his trousers; he slapped his head two or three times, much too hard; Charles looked up blankly and suddenly he howled, a timid wail at first, followed by bawling. Papa put his fingers in his ears.

'Be quiet at once! Have you forgotten your sister's dead?'

Olivier came in in his turn, barefoot, tousled with sleep;

he saw Charles being punished and to defend him he said, pulling down the corners of his mouth:

'I don't give a damn if she *is* dead.'

No one dared to breathe, we were looking at Papa. Papa filled with silence, his hands went limp, he began to cry again, quietly this time. He kissed us as he does on the days when he loves us most and calls us 'my dear ones'.

Henriette pushed open the door, she was buttoning the overall she wears for bathing Olivier and Charles; when she saw us she dissolved in tears, pressing her hands to her face.

Papa smiled a bit. 'You loved Claire too, didn't you, Henriette?'

'I can't believe it,' Henriette sobbed. 'I can't believe it, monsieur.'

Papa shook his head from side to side as horses do. He finished by saying, without looking at us:

'This morning Claire has black marks on her fingers.'

We got dressed very quietly. Even Olivier and Charles didn't say a word. At breakfast there was only the sound of cups clinking on saucers and we went downstairs with Papa in orderly fashion, taking care not to make any noise.

It was the day before July 14th. Already people were hanging flags on their balconies, the florists were watering the pots of flowers on the pavements and the water made twirling patterns in the dust.

It was still early at the clinic; the vases of flowers on the floor had not been taken into the rooms; the nuns were wearing their white habits for the night office, they were finishing their prayers silently, their lips moving, so they could not say good-morning.

There were no flowers outside Claire's door. Papa pushed

it half open and we slipped in one by one. Mother rose silently, she touched each of us on the shoulder as if she were counting us. She wasn't crying, she had a smell of stone. She pulled up the blind a little, she said she didn't dare open the window too wide because of the marks.

'Look, Jérôme, there's a new one on her chin.'

We gathered round Claire's bed, we looked for the marks, pretending not to. Small round marks. Purple. Not black. Olivier and Charles hadn't seen Claire before. Olivier leaned on the edge of the mattress, he stood on tiptoe, he opened his mouth wide but he didn't say anything. Papa picked Charles up. He held him over Claire.

Mother said: 'No, Jérôme, he's still too young.'

'I want him to remember,' Papa answered.

Charles stretched out his hands towards Claire's face, he gave her a damp kiss. Papa put him down again; Charles sighed, he looked at us all, he turned back to Claire and he clutched the sheet to climb on to the bed.

'Don't touch, baby,' Papa said.

Claire had stiffened, you could tell.

Papa pushed Olivier forward. 'Don't you want to kiss Claire?'

Olivier shook his head violently and retreated to the wall. 'Kiss Claire,' Papa said, overwrought. 'All of you kiss her.'

We couldn't. Claire had begun to flow towards the centre of the earth. Her face had the laxness of overblown flowers which are going to fall. We were afraid of Claire.

'One last time,' Papa insisted.

He dragged Valérie by the neck, she resisted.

'You mean you don't want to?'

Valérie said, 'Yes, I want to.' But she didn't move.

Mother seemed to come to, she said calmly:

'Let them alone, Jérôme, they're right, it isn't healthy.'

Mother wages relentless war on germs. At home, when an outsider uses the telephone, she's disinfecting the receiver with a rag dipped in eau-de-Cologne almost before he's hung up.

We looked at Mother, not understanding. And then undoubtedly we all thought of those stories you hear, worms in the grave and all that; we flung ourselves on Claire, we kissed her fervently, fiercely. 'Claire, don't ever go rotten, *please.*' We began to bellow, it was still a way of keeping Claire, of calling Claire.

The nun came in at once. 'Will you please be quiet. You can be heard right at the end of the corridor.'

Towards midday she (the nun) explained, 'It's due to this heat. If you wait any longer you're courting trouble.'

She had fastened her veil back with a pin, beads of sweat glistened on her forehead and nose, she didn't look old. She gathered up the saucer of water, the boxwood and the two candles. I helped her carry it all into the corridor, and I asked her:

'Do the lilies stay?'

She replied that the lilies belonged to the room next door. She walked quickly, and her leather shoes squeaked.

When I had my appendix out they put me on a trolley, covered me with a white sheet, and wheeled me along the corridors. I was laughing and saying 'Faster, Faster'. I was dizzy.

That's what they did with Claire. Two male attendants came with a trolley which they pushed alongside Claire's bed. They lifted her by her shoulders and her feet; Claire's body didn't sag in the middle, it stayed straight like a stem, and they made it slide.

We had withdrawn to the back of the room to leave space for the trolley. Papa and Mama had stationed themselves in front to prevent us seeing. Papa had both arms round Mother, and Mother said, 'Gently, oh, gently . . .' when they let Claire fall. The nun was busying herself stripping the mattress, unbuttoning the pillow-case; she whispered, shaking her fingers:

'Spread out a bit, don't look like a funeral procession.'

We didn't answer. Mother was leaning over Claire at the head of the trolley; she had the expression she wears when we are ill and she says, 'Go to sleep, Mother's here, she's going to make it all better.'

And it's true. We wake up refreshed, Mother hasn't moved, we are still hugging her hand to our heart. She has a surprise ready, apricots or a doll dressed up as a nurse. Mother caressed Claire's cheek before the nun drew the sheet over her face. Papa carried Charles, who doesn't walk fast enough, and we set off down the corridor. The nun skipped ahead, her habit swept the floor, other nuns pressed against the wall and crossed themselves as we passed. The attendants wheeled the trolley into the lift and we went down on foot, except for Mother who didn't let go of the iron handle.

We came out into the garden. Above the banks of flowers the sun was so high that you couldn't tell if the sky was blue or white, the breeze carried a scent of tar and sand. The trolley moved over the gravel with difficulty, Claire jerked about, and Mother put her hand on Claire's clasped ones, you could see the hump quite plainly under the sheet.

'I'm thirsty, Mama, I want a drink,' Olivier grumbled.

Mother said very quietly: 'In a minute.'

We arrived in front of the Annexe, a small, single-storeyed building standing on its own. Men dressed in black with striped trousers were waiting for us. They bared their heads and beckoned the trolley forward, as you signal a car to back into the garage. Inside, it smelt pleasant and fresh. There were masses and masses of flowers, gladioli, carnations, lilies, roses, marguerites, white flowers piled everywhere in sheaves and wreaths, even on the black and white tiles of the floor. Wicker chairs were ranged round the walls, like in a vestry. Alain was there, he stood very straight, his stomach pulled in and his hands crossed over it, you would have thought he was holding in the hiccups. He looked at the trolley, he towered over Claire, and then he closed his eyes. The men opened a double door, we saw a shining room painted green, and a coffin on trestles. But Claire isn't that big. We knew immediately that it was a coffin, a piece of furniture too obviously new, like a sideboard from the Galeries Barbès. Valérie blinked her eyes and two tears squeezed out on to her cheeks. The attendants thrust Papa, Mama and Alain inside and shut the door in our faces.

We stayed standing there to listen to what was going on behind it, the flap of sheets, the trolley creaking again, scrapings on the stone, the grunts of the removal men, a voice which said, 'Careful, there!'

Charles was sucking his thumb. The attendants came out with the empty trolley, they nodded to us by way of greeting and went away on tiptoe.

Papa came tremulously to the door, he told us to come in. Mother had her back to us, Papa touched her to indicate that we were there and she shook him off, without looking at us. Alain was holding his breath, he didn't look at us either.

No one could kiss Claire any longer. The deep-buttoned sides were too high. I don't know whether it was the men in black or the attendants who had been busy with Claire, but she had become like she used to be. The bandages round her head had been removed, her hair was free again, she was wearing her white wedding-dress. It should have been forbidden to look at Claire as if she were merely asleep, shut up in a satin casket like in the belly of a whale.

I suppose one is always stupid in the presence of the dead. Farewell, Claire, a long farewell, as Papa said. Go faster, farther, since it is pointless for you to linger. Go away before we are ashamed.

The men in black asked Papa if they could go. Papa bowed his head, they lifted the lid, put it in position on the casket, brought out a burner from a bag, one of them put on a transparent mask. And they soldered Claire in.

When the blue sparks began Mother suddenly dragged us outside. In the sun she tidied her hair – she has short hair, brown and blonde at once – she held out a hand each to Olivier and Charles and she said:

'Now we're going to go and have a lovely lunch. You'd like that, wouldn't you?'

Claire came with us. She joined us down the path edged with box. She was wearing a low-necked yellow silk sweater, black flared trousers, Italian gold sandals. Her hair flowed down over her arms, her footsteps made no sound on the gravel. The sun had become overpowering. I breathed so deeply that it lit up my lungs, two dark ruby caverns, and I danced a few steps. Valérie pinched me, she whispered:

'Are you crazy?'

The heat sent shudders down us. On coming out of Claire's garden-house all this white sudden sun was dazzling. Papa walked with his hands clasped over his face, like Adam driven out of Eden in my book of religious history. I've tried it, you can see quite well between your fingers. Alain's parents came towards us . . . the old gentleman was pushing his wife with difficulty, the wheels were sinking in the gravel.

The old lady is so fat that she will never get up again. She lives in a chair with a bicycle-chain which can be wheeled even up and down stairs. When she gets bored she knocks on the ceiling with her stick and has slices of bread and butter spread with foie gras sent up to her.

She says her waist used to be so small that Claire wouldn't be able to get into her wedding corset. Her eyes were weeping blue tears. She wanted to kiss us, so did the old gentleman. Usually Mother doesn't like him to, he has a sore on his lip, you never know, it might be cancer.

They told us that they loved Claire very much. In speaking of her they called her 'your poor sister'. they said they supposed we must be very unhappy. Especially Mother. The old gentleman patted Mother and, turning to Papa, he suggested that, despite it all, there was something worse than losing one's child: losing one's husband.

The old lady protested; she said, 'Oh no, Fernand, no!'

Alain's father put his hand on the frame of his glasses to take them off. In the midst of our silence we heard the birds, they were singing much more loudly than usual. Mother made a movement towards Papa to take his hand. And

Claire passed among us. Papa had an air of utter incredulity, his eyes were full of tears. Alain's mother stretched out her neck towards Mother and breathed:

'Luckily you've still got four, Véronique.'

'Please!' Mother said faintly.

If Claire has tawny hair and full lips which don't quite cover her top teeth, then I saw her.

It was not a lovely lunch as Mother had promised, it was noodles, noodles just like we have in September when we go back to school in the rain, with the smell of damp text-books. Mother made Olivier and Charles have a bath and get into their pyjamas. In mid-afternoon, of all things! We lunched on the bare table, without a cloth, it was the first time.

With my forehead on the table, I played at being a horse who is going to be finished off with a revolver bullet.

Valérie said: 'Oh, stop trying to be interesting.'

Abruptly she burst into tears. The sounds she produced seemed to come from her stomach. Mother looked at us. You could see she wanted to love us, but no one would have dared touch her, and besides, she hadn't even heard Valérie snivelling. Papa wasn't taking any notice of us, either. He was munching petit-beurres which he dipped in bitter orange marmalade, as on the days when his digestion's playing up. As a rule Mother says to him:

'You're getting just like your poor father.'

Claire was Grandfather's favourite. He always took her with him when he went to Châtelguyon for a cure and she played roulette in the Casino and he gave her the emerald clips which had belonged to Grandmother No. 1. He used to say to Claire, 'You can sit on my knee so long as you're under eighteen.' And even when she was eighteen he continued to say to her 'so long as you're under eighteen'. Grandfather won't have the pleasure of being grief-stricken, he's dead. I remember it very well because it was my birthday and I didn't get a present. Grandfather was lying almost sitting up in bed and he was breathing with a sort of pear-shaped rubber bulb which whistled. Mother sent us to the Bois with Henriette, and when we got back he was dead. In the end we were told and Aunt Rebecca took us to the country and we ate french fries every day until Mother arrived and made Olivier, Charles and me take a spoonful of castor oil each. She put two chamber-pots in the corners, I was on the throne, as Henriette calls it, and all morning the three of us amused ourselves by making as many noises as possible, it was a competition to see who could imitate Grandfather the best. Olivier and I had found a name for referring to Grandfather without anyone realizing; it was Pompom II, after a cat we used to have who always had colic, like him.

And then there was a procession of people up the big red staircase where the mirrors reach right to the ceiling. They rang one by one, they had put on their black, and their mourning voices whispered against the walls as they do in an empty house.

Mother had been taken ill after lunch. She had adopted the attitude of a figure on a tomb, lying in Papa's big bed with her eyes turned up to the ceiling. Papa was rubbing her ankles with one hand and she was shivering and crying, 'What ever is it?'

The callers were intrigued by Mother's illness, they asked to see her, they leaned against the door-jamb for a moment.

they looked at her, shaking their heads, and they withdrew on creaking soles. They creaked like this all along the corridor, looking round cautiously as if they were likely to be ambushed. They regained their voices only in the shelter of Papa's study.

I sat opposite them, serious, I hope, awaiting their questions. To make herself useful, Grandmother Cartet had shut Olivier and Charles in the dining-room. She was knitting and rocking to and fro, her mauve hair fluffed out against the saffron-yellow curtains. Olivier and Charles were pretending to be trucks under the table, but very quietly, as if they had only two gears. I don't know what we were waiting for. Anything, a pipe among the reeds. We no longer felt distress, but our words, our gestures, were governed by a sort of prudence which counselled us to silence and secrecy.

Mme Humbert and Mme Sarthe, their husbands and unmarried daughters in tow, gave a short, discreet ring. I ran down the hall to be first at the door and then I slowly opened one half of the double door and looked them in the eye. They said, 'Poor little girl . . .' and I drew back before they could touch my chin or my cheek. I led them into Papa's study, I settled one lady in the gold velvet armchair which smells of dust, and the others sat, hands on knees, on delicate Empire chairs which force everyone to sit very straight. I sat under the twin portraits of Marshal Pétain and General de Gaulle, and my legs looked too bare, my pink-and-green-striped frock too bright. I couldn't somehow imagine that disaster had struck us and that people were coming to offer their sympathy in the expectation that we would do the same for them when their turn came.

They say that lepers' skin loses all feeling, that they can

burn themselves and know nothing about it until their eyes register it and so they learn of their injury.

I'm afraid I am a leper, I never feel anything. From time to time this makes me uneasy and I score my thighs with a razor-blade. I look at these big red lines under my skirt and I am rather proud. Mother saw them one day when I sat down and my skirt billowed out. She kissed me rather emotionally and I heard her telling Grandma that I was mortifying myself. I did not understand what was so serious about Claire's death. She wasn't around, but that was not unusual.

The callers didn't manage to conceal their disappointment at seeing only me instead of a more sizeable sample of our stricken family. Nevertheless, I offered some degree of interest because they didn't know me, all during these years I was at boarding-school. I didn't look sad enough, they looked at me censoriously – my legs too bare, my frock too bright – someone ought to have scolded me, perhaps. They kept wanting to see my father. Papa was busy with the undertakers. And my mother? I took them for a glimpse of Mother lying down.

'And your poor sister?' they enquired.

Valérie had gone out to do some funeral shopping. So then they wanted to hear how Claire died.

We know it all by heart. On Sunday morning Claire left to go and see some friends. Which friends? I don't know Claire's friends. She was known to be alone, witnesses saw her. She came down a hawthorn-bordered path on her bicycle, letting go of the handlebars. Claire always lets go of the handlebars on a bike. She said hallo to someone. She said goodbye to him several times.

According to witnesses, she arrived rather fast at the crossing with the highway. The car which was going to kill her, not yet in sight, came out of a side road and ignored the stop sign. That was when the man at the wheel saw Claire, he told the police. He was a pig-farmer, that is, a pig-salesman.

'Pigs?' said Mme Sarthe. 'How dreadful!'

He saw Claire make a wide sweep and go over the crossing. At first he thought he would pass on Claire's left, according to the highway code. Then he thought it as well to swerve to the right to allow Claire time to get to the far side. At that moment Claire saw him. She hesitated. To the right. To the left. They were still far apart, almost directly opposite. There was no danger, everything was going fine. At that point the crossing with the highway is as big as the forecourt of a church. They were alone, Claire on her bicycle and the pig-salesman in his 245 h.p. Chevrolet. Witnesses said that they never stopped stalking each other, zigzagging forward like two pedestrians colliding on the pavement while trying to take avoiding action.

The car's offside fender caught Claire. Claire went flying over the hood and landed broken. So did the bicycle.

'What happened next?' said Mme Humbert.

I invented. Claire was not in any pain. She was merely puzzled to find herself stretched out on the ground. She even observed to the pig-salesman with a nervous little smile:

'It doesn't seem as if I've broken anything. I was scared.'

But she could not move her head. Naturally not, with a broken neck. So she did not see the blood which was spreading under her, under her shoulders, under her doubled-up leg. The pig-salesman was leaning over her, he was very red, he mopped his forehead, when he spoke little white bubbles formed at the corners of his mouth. The people on the café terrace hurried over and the pig-salesman said to them:

'What a mess, oh, what a mess, this is going to cost me a pile.'

Claire complained of pain in her head.

The pig-salesman said: 'But she must have been out of her mind.'

He examined the paint on his front offside fender, which was hardly scratched. While he did so Claire's gaze went blank and no one in the world knows what she could have been thinking. Except me.

First she fell backwards down a stairwell fresh and feather-filled. When her fall ended, she was lying very comfortably and she knew that she was going to die. She cried a bit, as children do when they are shut up in the dark but aren't really frightened. She was sorry for herself, she was sorry for our parents, but not for us: she knew perfectly well that there is no love lost between brothers and sisters when they are young. She didn't think of Alain at all. She was sorry for the sky and for all the sunrises to come, but she was very soon reconciled to dying.

Mme Humbert began to cry. She really cried, not just out of politeness, she got up, she took me in her arms, and I realized that sorrow is the beginning of love for what is unknown.

And then I had had enough of telling people about Claire. I didn't want to answer any more when someone rang at the door.

Grandma said: 'But, my pet, you were enjoying it so much just now.'

Olivier and Charles were on all fours under the table, they weren't playing at anything now, they were peering under Grandma's skirt.

We heard Papa's key in the lock and we ran towards him to get away from Grandma. Papa was in black now, he was no longer like us. He gave us a bristly kiss, he tucked Olivier under one arm and Charles under the other and he dumped them on Mother, in her bed. Mother didn't open her eyes, she hugged the boys to her. Charles pressed himself against her and began to suck his thumb. Grandma followed, she wanted to reclaim Olivier and Charles.

Grandma can never leave us alone. If we are sitting in an armchair, even if there are four others empty, she says:

'Aren't you going to get up and let Granny have your chair?'

Claire shakes her head and her hair dances like snakes. In the country she climbs out of the attic window on to the roof. She walks along the ridgepole, spreading her arms wide like wings, she calls: 'Grandma . . . yoo-hoo . . .'

Grandma used to come out on to the lawn in front of the house, she would manage with difficulty to twist her neck upwards.

'Have the goodness to come down at once. At once, do you hear?'

Claire laughs, and the echo laughs also. Grandma would get cross.

'You'll end up killing yourself at that game.'

Claire says it's all the same to her. Grandma shrugged.

'A fine lot of good you'll be when you're dead.'

'A fine lot more than you,' says Claire.

The day dragged on endlessly, like light when you look at it through the narrow end of a funnel. In the evening we had a dress rehearsal without Claire. That is to say, all the people recently involved were there, Alain, his father and mother, our grandmother, and all of us, except Claire of course. Everyone was in formal dress; even I had on a black frock. I don't want to fail in respect towards Claire, but I was pleased. I looked quite the young lady, from a distance. I looked at myself solemnly in the big mirrors in the hall and Alain said:

'You're almost ready to go dancing next year, now.'

Valérie made a face. 'The stupid clod will walk all over their feet.'

Alain stroked my cheek. 'It won't be for her feet that the boys will ask her.'

I took Alain's hand, put it round my shoulders and held myself against him and we stared at Valérie until she went away. And then Alain crouched down in front of me, he held me at arm's length, I saw his freckles and his eyes all soft. My blood was pounding in my ears, Claire was there, close at hand, as in fairy-stories you mustn't turn round or she would vanish.

'Do you realize you look like her?' Alain said.

'Oh no,' I said, with great hope.

Alain touched my face all over with his finger. 'Eyebrows, forehead, nose . . .'

'Legs,' I said very quickly, 'legs and hands.'

'And what's going to be in there later on?' Alain said, touching my forehead.

Without meaning to, I replied: 'A girl who's dead.'

45

I was very upset. Alain hugged me to him, repeating 'Hush, hush.' I asked him:

'Do you still love Claire, Alain?'

'Of course,' Alain said, 'of course, you'll forget, as we all shall.'

'Will you still get married?'

'Look,' Alain said, 'we're all overwrought at the moment.'

I shrugged. They wear me out, making such a to-do about death. I dragged Alain into my room to show him a secret no one else knows about, my Vietnam soldiers. I cut them out of *Paris-Match*, I've got eleven of them, they sleep in every conceivable attitude, with blood on their faces.

Alain put on a parental expression. 'It's very bad to be so morbid, you'd do better to play with your dolls.'

I explained to him that my soldiers were much better than dolls. They were living dead. Like Claire.

Dinner was a very pious meal. It was Grandma who began it. She buried her nose in her mushroom soup and murmured:

'The Lord looked upon her, and loved her, and took her to Himself.'

Claire's ex-future parents-in-law replied politely: 'Amen.'

Mother was being embarrassing again; she kept smiling all the time. Her lips were swollen and she spoke only with her eyes, by which I mean that she offered the food without speaking but you guessed she was imagining herself saying the words. So we just whispered 'Thank you very much' so as not to disturb her. Papa wasn't eating. He sat hunched over his plate and stared at the salt-cellar. At one point he began to hum a little song Claire used to sing sometimes. And then he looked at us without seeing us, and fell silent.

We didn't know what to do with ourselves. Olivier was kicking the table, you couldn't see anything but his crew-cut. Valérie kept giving him dirty looks but she didn't dare be mean because of making a good impression on Alain. The old lady and Grandma were reckoning up the number of days' indulgence they had procured for Claire by saying certain special prayers.

'Not that she has any need of them,' Grandma concluded. 'She is an angel among the angels.'

During the meat course Grandma checked with Mother that Henriette wasn't going to be at the funeral. She would be sure to sob too loudly and people might think she was family. Between the saffron-yellow curtains the sky was violet blue.

'Tomorrow there will be rejoicing in Heaven over Claire,' said the old gentleman.

Please, God, don't let there be any Paradise, let prayers be so much bunk, and let us be delivered from others when we are dead.

While we were eating cheese Claire was unstiffening, soldered into the airless box, and her chin would form a sharper and sharper angle with her neck, to the point where a broken line, visible at last, joined it to her nape and the ring of small bones forming the spinal column.

I am always top in anatomy. I prefer this integral view of our bodies, the skeleton, to the garniture of our flesh. I have given my Vietnam soldiers high-sounding names, they are called Radius, Cubitus, Humerus, Trochanter, you would think they were the names of Roman emperors. Claire has embarked on the easiest of all adventures. Later on we shall be the same age and I shall know her secrets.

I never cry, it's easy, it's just a matter of curling your toes up in your shoes. I didn't take any Roquefort because of possible worms. Mother had the beaming look of someone filled with joy: 'At six, Claire adored Camembert,' she said. That's it. For Mother, Claire is again becoming a little girl who loses her first milk tooth and hides it under her pillow so that the good fairy will change it into a present. Soon, for Mother, Claire will be her newborn second child, and soon after Mother will prefer to be pregnant with Claire and to dream of hopes as long as life. Mother says she is never so happy as when she has a baby in her arms. The trouble is that as we grow bigger we become a nuisance and she has to put us down on the ground.

Tomorrow Mother is going to put Claire down in the ground.

Papa loves us collectively, not as individuals. For him we are one child divided into four, plus Claire. So on the morning of Claire's funeral he took no notice of us, except to get mad at Valérie, who had borrowed his razor to shave her legs. He was ready much too soon and he spent the extra time in closing the shutters of the flat and fastening the windows behind the drawn curtains; he also turned off the gas and electric meters, as if we were going away for a long time.

He was wearing the outfit he would have worn for leading Claire to the altar, and a pearl pin stuck in his grey tie. He had cut himself under the chin and Mother put sticking plaster on it, she said she would take it off just before we got to the clinic.

Mother was beautiful. She was no longer our everyday Mother. She was very tall, transparent behind her black veils, with a face like a flower, two steady blue petals for her eyes and a bright burning petal for her mouth. We couldn't kiss her. She inspected us in the hall before leaving. All our shoes were shining. Olivier was wearing his first communion trousers and a black armband over his shirt. Charles was crying quietly because he was wearing rompers with white shoulder-straps and he wanted trousers like Olivier's, but Mother told him white was the Chinese colour of mourning and he was happy.

I don't know how to put it, but we were not a family that morning, we could neither touch one another nor speak.

In the entrance to the block the concierges and the local tradespeople had assembled for a good look at us. The main doorway was draped in black with our initial on the pediment and I was ashamed, as if our home was marked with a sign of infamy. Mother and Father left with Grandma, who had already got into the car, carefully settled by Henriette, her black plumes very straight on her hat and all. We followed in Aunt Rebecca's car, a cheerful car which always has papers and sweets and magazines all over the place. On the main road, she enquired if we had thought to go to the lavatory, because the ceremony would be a long one. She also suggested croissants, she was sure we didn't have anything in our stomachs, but we didn't want greasy crumbs. Noses pressed to the window, we gazed at the oatfields, the geometrical aeroplanes, and everything was very far away. We were a bit cold despite the mounting heat, and when we happened to yawn tears blurred our view.

There were so many cars below Claire's clinic that we had to walk the rest of the way.

'Nothing like a fine day for a successful funeral,' Aunt
Rebecca said, 'in novels as in real life. When it rains, people
don't bother to turn up.'

She waved right and left to acknowledge her friends.
Everyone wanted to see us but we were in a hurry to rejoin
Mother and Father and we walked very fast, with our heads
down.

They were our darling little parents, they were holding hands and we lined up behind them, and then the
coach arrived: a white coach drawn by four horses, three
whites and a black. Mother stifled a cry with her hand; she
said:

'No, Jérôme, not a black, it's impossible.'

Papa went and parleyed with the fine coachmen, they
shook their heads a long time and in the end one of them
went back into the Annexe where they had put Claire two
or three days earlier. He returned with a saddle-cloth for
the horse. And the black horse became white.

'That's good,' Mother said.

She turned round to us; she said: 'I love you, I love you,
I love you.'

And without moving we leapt towards her, we hoped to
be a litter of kangaroos enfolded in her pouch, but we didn't
say anything because we had vowed, even Charles, to be
dignified. Mother had asked us the night before on coming
to tuck us up. She would have preferred us not to come to the
funeral, to have merely thought of Claire from time to
time during our games by day, during our dreams by
night, without distress, without sorrow. She spoke to us
quietly so that people couldn't hear; she said again:

'You're my wonderful children, I'm so lucky to have
you. I'm so lucky that one of you is already in Heaven.'

And then we heard the silence. We had not noticed the
silence until the men in black brought out Claire's coffin.
They placed it in the coach and they formed a chain from
the door of the Annexe to pass out the wreaths. Lilies,
marguerites, gladioli, white roses. Especially lilies. A super-
abundance of lilies. You could have made garlands for the
horses and strewn the rest on the ground to make a path of
flowers, like in the Hosanna story.

Alain came forward all alone, severely black, he was
carrying Claire's wedding bouquet in his arms and he
placed it on top of the pile, then he came to stand beside
us.

Far behind us, people began to shuffle forward, we knew
without turning round because the sound of their feet was
different when they reached the gravel.

The moment had come. An usher separated us, Papa,
Olivier, Charles and Alain in one row behind the coach,
Mother, Valérie and me in the second row. Grandma and
Alain's old parents weren't with us, Papa had said their
legs wouldn't last out and Aunt Rebecca was driving them
by car.

The horses pulled forward and the load of flowers shook.
We walked as if there was music, very slowly, with much
ceremony everywhere, in the sun and the swaying of the
coach and the white horses and in our light hearts which
were discovering the true life. Claire did not make the
flowers burst, but she kindled the sun beneath our feet.
Mother was right, we ought to have formed a circle and

laughed round the coach, and then we should have had a battle with the flowers, we should have tossed them over our heads, and when the coffin was exposed we should have wakened Claire by force, we should have taken it in turns to lie down in this sort of satin casket and it would have been great fun. Often, when everyone is asleep, Olivier, Charles and I play at being dead. The corpse lies down quietly, we cover him with a sheet and we light four candles at the corners of the bed. Another candle is placed on his stomach, and if the flame flickers he isn't really dead and we torture him by pinching and scratching him in those places where it hurts when you're alive. If he is really dead, we kiss him tenderly, stroke his hair and recite to him:

'How happy art thou now thou art in security. We make thee free of every place that the sole of thy foot shall tread, from the desert to the mighty ocean beneath the setting sun.'

Behind his quivering eyelids, you can see the dead person is pleased.

On top of the hill the church bells began to toll, a clay-coloured sound, deep as a volcano, and I felt sick with happiness. The coach was swaying its load of flowers, the horses were almost dancing, and Papa took Olivier and Charles by the hand. I knew Mother's lips were trembling in a smile.

To live and then die marvellously like Claire under her flowers. The telephone wires rose and fell, the trees grew tall before tottering, and the dust of the road rose in luminous layers and the horse on the right lifted his head joyfully and neighed. I turned round, the cortège, more or less black, dragged in the heat and on the long road the cars glided slowly, one by one. It was a shame we had to trail all those people behind us.

The double doors of the church were open on the emptiness within. We could no longer draw back. The horses had deposited golden dung at the foot of the steps. The fine coachmen took off their hats again, moved the flowers to one side, and Claire was carried in triumph up to the altar, and the organ music was like a crowd's applause. We were placed on the prie-dieux of honour, Papa, Olivier, Charles and Alain on one side, Mother, Valérie, Aunt Rebecca and me on the other, plus Grandma, who had hobbled up the long central aisle to join us.

The choirboys adjusted the silver chain of the censer, and when the sound of people piling in among the pews had subsided, the punishment began.

They wove circles around Claire by means of prayers and incense, they made the music soar like a second vault of stone, and they called on God so loudly that we got goose-flesh.

Grandma said we were going to catch a chill after the sun outside, but if she really died it was overdue in any case. I dreamed a bit that it was Grandma lying in place of Claire under the white trappings, and I very much wanted to cry.

Looking to the side as only horses are able to do, I saw Mother blinking far above the candles and the little flames reflected in her eyes. Grandma was telling her beads, she always prays haphazardly, she says her rosary at Mass and reads the Mass in her bedroom. Olivier and Charles were frightfully dignified, it must have made their necks ache. Valérie was pulling the face she pulls when she thinks she's being beautiful, she was biting the insides of her cheeks so as to have interesting hollows in her jaw.

Valérie loathes us. She hid Claire's first evening dress under her mattress and Claire couldn't go out with Alain for the first time, and she yelled, 'It isn't fair, it isn't fair,' and she even rushed out into the street without a coat, sobbing brokenly, and Mother caught up with her on the pavement and slapped her to make her get back into the house.

Now, Claire has been brought down from the coach while the horse on the left, the one with swellings on its legs, lowered its head majestically and the one on the right tossed its mane joyfully and neighed.

Now, if I were a young man, I should say to Claire: 'Henceforth you are pale and I love you.'

And Claire would come forth from the shadows, she would appear sovereign virgin, living Jerusalem, beauty of Israel, hope in darkness, and each morning of misery, each evening of anguish, we should repeat how happy we were, how good was our portion. That's what Canon Maillart told us. He told us to kneel, and we kept vigil over Claire who was making us suffer.

They asperged her to the four points of the compass and they made a corpse out of her. There is no other explanation. The Canon told us once more to thank God for the good He was sending us while keeping politely quiet about the ill from which He had not preserved us.

Then the organ pealed forth again and the usher with his staff conducted us down the side-aisle and people queued up to congratulate us on the success of the ceremony and on Claire having become a hard white thing in a coffin.

Alain was the only one to look people in the face, to intersperse their words of sympathy with gestures of resignation – I even heard him reply to Mme Humbert that God's will be done. Valérie gazed at him with drowned eyes, as if he had promised her recompense after Claire's death.

We remained dignified right to the end, but unhappiness rose in us because everyone was praying that we should be unhappy. There was no need to think of Claire beneath the white draperies. Too late. Too late – that is what these people wanted as they breathed 'Be brave' in our faces and insisted on kissing us willy-nilly. Even Charles realized it, he grew frightened, he began to yell for Mother. Mother didn't answer, she couldn't because of keeping her dignity; so Charles – he must have sensed it was forbidden – shrieked, 'Claire, Claire . . .'

I kicked him; Valérie said to him, 'Be quiet, she's coming back' – anything to make him shut up. The people within earshot were deeply moved.

When the last stragglers had filed past, Papa lifted Mother's black veil, he took her face between his hands and kissed her, like on their wedding-day, in the photograph where he is putting back her white veil and she is looking fixedly at his mouth.

In another photograph Father and Mother are standing with their arms round each other on the terrace in the country, they are laughing and Papa has captioned it: 'And Baby makes three.' Apparently Mother is expecting Claire in this photograph, but Claire is completely invisible.

Outside, at the foot of the steps, the coach had disappeared and so had the horses and the coachmen. We came out of the church orphans, even Father and Mother, and in the sunlight we looked poor, you saw it in the expressions of the people clustered on the forecourt who were whispering about us behind our backs.

The coffin was shoved into a hearse with the minimum of flowers, plus Father and Mother in front, the doors were slammed and off they drove. Alain followed with his old parents. The poor fat lady had been waiting all this time in the car because her wheelchair hadn't been brought, but they had left her a packet of petit-beurres and she had had a good munch.

We got back in with my aunt and lots of other cars drove off in their turn. Thus we left in a long procession behind Claire, heading for another district which we didn't know, where the former members of our family are buried, our two grandfathers and Grandmother No. 1.

It seems that to make room for Claire it had been necessary to decant Grandmother into Grandfather. There was nothing left of our young grandmother but the old-fashioned folds of the blue gown in which they dressed her when my father was born, which is when she died. In the fresh air they fluttered into dust and, except for her little jawbone, there was nothing to put beside Grandfather but a pinch of memories. Papa told Mother about it in front of us. All the better for Claire, all the more reason for hope, if it is true that we become nothing but a shuddering breath and not creatures shut up for evermore beneath the vault of a garden.

That is what I was thinking of, as I stared fixedly at the hearse which was carrying Claire squeezed into the box. Claire indifferent and lost, her pale hair folded under her nape and her body stretched out in her wedding-dress, jouncing over the bumps in the road.

Claire and her pointless injuries. Claire who had plunged into the unknown with one almighty somersault over the hood of a car. Behind my close-shut lids I called to her with all my strength:

'Claire, kill me. I too want to live on the scale of the universe, I too want to grow up and run away, Claire, Claire . . .'

And I felt her warm around me, on my face, my bare arms, she began to move very gently in my stomach, my aunt braked sharply, I bent double in the grass and bitter, burning waves came out of my mouth and I listened to everything I had just missed hearing and which is for ever incommunicable.

Since then, every time I think too much about Claire, I am sick. Valérie says I ought to go around in an apron. She's jealous that it doesn't happen to her.

After I had been ill on the grass verge, we all felt better. Aunt Rebecca made me go in front, under Grandma's sharp elbow, and she let me have a puff of her cigarette to take away the taste. She inhales deeply when she smokes and the tube of ash extends delicately, then spills on to her sweaters. She drives like racing drivers, lying under the steering-wheel, the wind blows her red hair into her eyes and two lovely wrinkles frame her smile.

She nearly had a husband who made off with her carpets and silver, that's all I know. Since then, she picks up hitch-hikers on the highway – I heard Mother talking about it to Grandma – and she is never asked to parties at our house.

She switched on the car radio and we heard guitars for happy people, people who would be hanging dessert cherries over their ears and drinking wine slowly under orange parasols.

'Turn it off,' yelped Valérie, 'you've no sense of decency.'

'Don't make me laugh,' said my aunt.

'Come, Rebecca,' Grandma said, 'respect the conventions.'

My aunt changed gear and, putting her foot down on the accelerator, overtook the line of cars which had passed us during our halt in the grass. Olivier and Charles woke up, they crouched over Valérie on all fours and went bim-bam, bim-bam at the tops of their voices, louder than the guitars, and the wind of journeys carried us up behind the hearse which was threading its way through open country. The sun was still sinking and waves of heat flowed over the tar. We were overawed once more.

'Let's get it over quickly,' Aunt Rebecca said.

As soon as she switched off the engine we were scared. We sensed at once that however much we might drag it out, there were only a very few minutes left in which Claire would still be among us.

The coffin had been unloaded. The Canon, carrying his crucifix, had already take up position among the graves. We didn't want to get out. Even Grandma had gone quiet. We could hear the grasshoppers and smell the sun-baked grass. Mother came across to us quite normally, though she looked preoccupied. She said Olivier, Charles and I were to stay in the car. We scrambled over Valérie and Grandma to get out, looked at Mother and shook our heads. Mother almost smiled. She hugged us and said:

'Now listen, this is nothing to get upset about, Mother says so. Is that clear?'

'That clear,' Charles echoed loudly.

Mother gave a little shove to propel us forward, and we advanced behind the coffin, not holding hands. The Canon raised his silver crucifix on high, and although we walked as tall as we possibly could, we were much smaller than usual. We longed to blot ourselves out against Mother and Father, but they were behind us.

When we came to the tomb, which was like a little house, we saw the hole where the slab had been removed, and the heap of earth.

The bier with the coffin upon it was set down. And after that I don't remember anything any more.

Except that Charles's teeth started to chatter and Mother held his jaw and hid his face against her skirt.

Except Papa's face as he stood on tiptoe to lean over the grave, while big tears ran down his cheeks and met under his chin.

White roots poking through the heap of earth.

The blue-and-whiteness of the sky, the dull black of mourning, the smell of incense.

One of the undertaker's men mopping his bald head with a handkerchief.

Our clothes getting stuffier and stuffier.

Someone in the crowd, unseen, unknown, beginning to sob loudly in our stead.

Canon Maillart's slow and stately blessing of this everlasting hide-out.

And then the rotten beast made us sing '*Ce n'est qu'un au revoir*' while the coffin bumped against the sides of the hole as the ropes were paid out.

And then Alain plighted himself to our whole family.

Head bowed before our parents, he swore that he was our

brother and their son; and he was the first to throw earth in upon Claire.

The Canon scares me. He's too kind. He talks to us only in a general way about ourselves in the future, with compliments which we don't deserve. It's very embarrassing.

Canon Maillart is the presiding genius of our family. He married my father and mother, he baptized us all, and so on. Every time he comes to lunch with us on Sundays, he suggests informally hearing our confessions. He settles himself in Papa's study, beneath the twin portraits of Marshal Pétain and General de Gaulle, and he makes us kneel opposite. Papa never goes. He drinks an Americano or mends a fuse while Mother is in there.

Valérie makes out her list of sins shielded by her elbow so that no one can copy from her. Claire . . . I no longer know what Claire does. I think she is in the kitchen teaching Henriette to dance and dipping her finger into the chocolate cream.

When it's Olivier's turn he speaks so loudly that we can hear him through the door. He recites at top speed:

'I deliberately broke the glass in the hall, I stole money from Mother's handbag . . .' and we thus discover who was responsible for misdeeds which have remained a mystery. It's a trick he has to avoid punishment.

From time to time the Canon seeks me out; he says, 'Our turn now.'

I reply that I've already been done at boarding-school. He looks at me and I no longer know where to put myself. He starts to laugh and his cross bobs about on his violet stock which is filling out more every year; he points at me and says:

'God will catch you as you're turning round, He'll make a great saint out of you.'

All this because I raised my head and opened my mouth of my own accord to receive the salt of wisdom, the day he baptized me.

Since then, God makes me thoroughly uneasy.

In the evenings I take a running jump from the door into my bed so that God doesn't catch me by the heels; I say to Him:

'Please, God, forget all about me, don't let me be a great saint.'

Once Claire surprised me at my prayers and she burst out laughing. Unfortunately she doesn't take me seriously. She's waiting for me to grow up. She stretches with a long, jerky movement, she pushes her hair back behind her ears, she yawns as cats do and the two small pointed teeth that she has at the back pierce her smile; she says:

'Hurry and grow up, so I can talk to you.'

And then she goes out, her feet in pink mules falling over each other without tripping. Her eyes are laughing over her shoulder when she turns round before opening the door, she brushes against me in passing but she doesn't ruffle my hair or anything. She doesn't touch me.

Claire and I don't kiss, nor shake hands, nor even greet each other. We're waiting till I grow up. We hardly know each other because I'm away at boarding-school and often in the vacations she goes off to places in the mountains or by rivers, I don't know, I never listen to what's being said around me, it isn't yet interesting.

When we meet, we don't look at each other. We observe each other a bit, as and when occasion arises, and I discover

that she has small square ears. She holds herself so tense that
you can sometimes see the delicate bones of her hips like
pebbles marking out the field of her belly. Or else she
measures my nose with a tape measure, then her own,
and says:

'You and I have the smallest noses in the family.'

And that is another sign between us.

It's because of Claire that I asked to go to boarding-school,
oh, ages ago. At boarding-school you have to eat and do
gymnastics, and that makes you grow quicker. You have to
work too, so you don't have to stay down so much and that
speeds up the time when you leave.

On my return from boarding-school in July, just before
Claire died, it was she who opened the door to me; she
fluttered her eyelids like a long-lashed doll; she said:

'Well! Who'd have thought it!'

I had grown two inches during the term and I hadn't
told anyone, and she spotted it at once.

'Well! Who'd have thought it!' – perhaps it was the
signal. That evening big-bellied moths blundered about
with sickening thuds, they were swallowed up, whirling,
under the red shade of my lamp; and with my legs drawn
up in bed and wearing those ridiculous pyjamas with
Pinocchios on them, I studied Claire.

Claire had opened our windows wide on the warmth of
the lime-trees, where the two owls whom we know well are
on the move. She brought out armfuls of her dresses and
things which she spread on her bed; she picked them up one
by one, held them against her, looked at herself in the glass,

biting her lip a bit. Then she cast them aside and murmured to herself:

'Not that one.'

She turned to me. 'You won't say anything, promise, swear?'

She felt in the hollow between her breasts for a blue telegram-form, she kissed it, she pressed it to her lips, she bit it, she tore it into little pieces with her teeth, she ended by swallowing the whole telegram, literally eating it.

She curled up on her bed like a cat; she recited:

'Ho and ha and tra-la-la, tick-tack-tock and ta-ra-ra . . .' words which made her laugh and cry. She said to the ceiling:

'Tomorrow, day of utt-er bliss. Afterwards, long mortal life with Bridegroom. Afterwards, only meetings with you every night in the Pole Star, at the tip of the Little Bear's tail.'

I understood perfectly well that Bridegroom was Alain, but I didn't ask about the rest.

And then Claire swept to the floor all the new dresses that Mother had bought her for her wedding to Alain, she put on her nightdress, she saluted herself several times in the glass, she whirled round and round like a white flame. She stopped in front of me, all out of breath; hand on heart, she repeated:

'Swear you won't say anything.'

I didn't answer. I pretended to be sleepy and I pulled the sheet up over my head as I said my prayer that makes me drop off: 'Please, God, forget all about me.'

In the morning Claire didn't want to waken me. She got dressed behind the shutters. She put on a tee-shirt and blue jeans. She spent an hour on her make-up. She was humming like someone whom things are going to happen to, and then she came close to my bed:

'Listen, you, don't pretend to be asleep. Tell Papa I've chosen the shell design for the silver spoons.'

That's all. She didn't say goodbye or anything. She went away and she is dead. She ought to have told me more, if it was really the signal when she said:

'Well! Who'd have thought it!'

Because I had grown up so much.

In the country it is still the same Sunday. Claire was born on October 8. So it was her nine hundred and seventy-sixth Sunday, only I hadn't yet worked it out.

Once again Mother went through all the rooms, opening and shutting doors, dabbing a finger on the mirrors to check that there was no dust.

Valérie was stretched out in the sun on a raffia mat, she had sheltered her remodelled nose under a roof of silver foil, she had stuffed a caramel into each cheek and she was reading *Elle* and sucking gently.

Olivier and Charles had secretly penetrated an African jungle on the lawn. They had brought a tiger back into the dining-room, and, faced with the heap of grass and twigs from the tiger, Henriette, who was sweeping, cried:

'I don't have two pairs of hands to clear up your mess.'

'Of course not,' Olivier said, 'if you had two pairs of hands you would have two brooms.'

Once again Mother called Claire all over the house, under the trees and even on the roof. With her clenched hands thrust deep in the pockets of her lacy housecoat, she said to Papa:

'She ought to be shut up, I tell you. Going off again

64

without warning, a mere two weeks before her wedding.'

Papa didn't listen to a word. He went on filling his ears with white lather and making complicated inroads upon his face with his razor.

Once again the young lady who plays the harmonium, young ever since we were born, with the same flat-chested flowered dress and the same delicate arched eyebrows, ran out of wind during the *Sanctus*.

Once again, coming out of Mass, Papa bought us some of those little cakes with writing on – 'I love you' or 'Out of sight, out of mind'.

Once again, and for the last time, as we sat down to table Mother railed at Claire, who would pay dearly for her escapade.

'You see if she doesn't,' Mother said, looking at us severely.

All this time Claire was travelling secretly towards her death. She was coming down a hawthorn-bordered path on her bicycle. Claire always lets go the handlebars on a bike. She said hallo to someone. She said goodbye to him several times. Witnesses saw her. She was laughing, her tawny hair streamed out behind her and the sun was on her laughter. Had she already fixed her rendezvous in the Pole Star? If so, someone is now very much alone in that star every night.

But from now on the end of the Pole Star for Claire was in the little tomb like a house. In there was her resting-place, the end of the countries of rivers or mountains, the end of her laughter when she had eaten the blue telegram-form.

'Oh, hold me tight, hug me tight . . .' Mother said to us

when the earth finished rattling down. We went back along the cemetery path between the box hedges and the people who were gradually finding their voices again and talking among themselves.

'Yes, terrible.'

'That poor boy! Did you know what to say to him?'

'Véronique ought to have a good cry or she'll break down.'

'Well, they had it coming to them, just like everyone else.'

'All the same, it's not as bad as having her crippled for life.'

'If you ask me, the girl had an easy death, one rabbit-punch and that was it. All over.'

'I wouldn't mind going the same way myself.'

'I say, hurry up, the taxi's turning.'

We had lost north, south, west. Papa looked like a man awakened in the middle of the night who sees that his fears were real. His good suit was wilted, but he was squaring his shoulders and pushing Olivier, Charles and me before him with a proprietary air.

Papa often calls us three youngest 'My second batch'.

And he gives us a complimentary wink. Papa is very polite to Valérie since she failed her *baccalauréat*. In the morning he enquires if she has slept well. He opens his wallet, holds out a note between thumb and forefinger and says to her, 'Don't thank me.'

If she asks permission to go and spend the Christmas holidays in Germany with an American girl-friend, he says without taking his moustache out of his coffee: 'Fix it with your mother.'

Mother leaves her hand on the coffee-pot for a whole hour.

'Suppose it's an American boy-friend, Jérôme?'

Papa shrugs his shoulders. 'What do you want me to do about it?'

'Suppose she comes back pregnant?'

'It'll give her something to do,' Papa replies.

Mother slams the door. If the noise of this doesn't upset Papa sufficiently, she starts all over again. Canon Maillart reassures Mother that Valérie will find her equilibrium in marriage.

'What else could she do?' Papa grumbles.

With Claire it's different. Papa puts on his grey suit and his pearl-grey tie, he crooks his arm to offer it to her, and he takes her to eat oysters. Aunt Rebecca says:

'Just look at those rascals living it up. At last I recognize Jérôme.'

It seems that before we came on the scene Papa was quite a gay dog, with a silver-mounted cane, always to be found at Maxim's, his eyes deep in the eyes of Lulu Diamant who used to drink champagne out of her cupped hand. The only flaw in Lulu Diamant was a small wart on the third finger of her left hand. And then Lulu Diamant married a poisonous banker who made her have her little wart removed. And Lulu Diamant died during the winter because her little wart was, all unbeknown, a sort of push-button which triggered off a cancer.

'For heaven's sake don't let your mother know I'm telling you all this,' Aunt Rebecca says.

Mother doesn't like it because Papa knew Aunt Rebecca before her. Papa says Mother has nothing to be afraid of,

Aunt Rebecca scared him far too much. She wanted to make Papa believe that she was alone in the world. That she had no family at the back of her. That she had no allowance at the back of her. That she had nothing at the back of her. Aunt Rebecca buys us chocolate éclairs, which Mother doesn't allow, she lights a fresh cigarette and the thread of smoke curls round her wrist, and we say:

'Tell us some more.'

We know it all by heart, but it's our favourite story.

'While your father was eating his heart out for Lulu Diamant, your mother was growing up between her silent father and her highly-strung, pious mother who is now your grandma.'

When she was twelve, Mother used to sit on her hair, she was fed on peas and bananas because it was the fashion for children to be plump. One day her German governess's ring split open her lip when she gave her a backhander for failing to obey an order. So the Fräulein was sent back to Germany and Mother was left with *Werther* imperfectly understood on her lap.

'When Lulu Diamant died, your mother was old enough to go to the opera in her father's box, with him in evening dress (he had managed to burn up his bronchial tubes through inhaling the cement in his workshops), and her mother who was already past the age for low-cut dresses. And I, who would have done better to break my leg that evening,' said Aunt Rebecca, 'I had dragged your father, inconsolable for Lulu Diamant, into the adjoining box.'

Olivier, Charles and I snuffled with happiness, we pushed aside the plate of chocolate éclairs, we waited until the waitress in her white apron had poured Aunt Rebecca a fresh cup of green tea with its smoky smell, and we said:

'And then?'

'Then . . .' said my aunt.

She took tiny, steaming sips, she left red lipstick-marks all round the cup, she did it on purpose to make us wait, beneath her mauve eyelids her eyes were laughing.

'Then your future father followed your future mother's car and he was mightily astonished to find she lived in the same block as I did. From the board in the hall he learnt that your grandfather was a building contractor. He went to consult him, and since your grandfather could not discover any serious intention of house-building on his part, your father ended up by saying that he was asking permission to build his daughter's happiness. 'Rebecca?' enquired your future grandfather. 'Not on your life,' replied your future father. 'Yes, I was surprised myself,' said your future grandfather. They met again, she in white, he in black, at Saint-Honoré d'Eylau, with the oral blessing of Canon Maillart and the written blessing of the Pope.

'Your father put away his silver-mounted cane, he no longer frequented Maxim's, he took to eating mashed potato to simplify the menus because Valérie was born.

'He had already given up being surprised at eating easily digested foods when Claire arrived, with a fresh blessing from the Canon. Your father was resigning himself to living indefinitely with the wet beds and six a.m. screamings to which Valérie had accustomed him, when he perceived that Lulu Diamant had returned in the sprawling, bawling person of Baby Claire.'

'Isn't Claire Mother's daughter?' Olivier asks.

'Ah,' sighs Aunt Rebecca, 'you're too sharp by half.'

She lifts a finger to signal for the bill, her gold bangles fall tinkling to her elbow, she gets out her lipstick, and we watch her draw in a gendarme's hat between her two lovely wrinkles.

At the cemetery gates we made a final halt for the final leave-taking. This time it was as though people were seeking some trace of Claire in our faces and wishing her a swift godspeed before the train pulled out.

Canon Maillart did his bit by shaking a lot of hands, and Papa's fellow-members of the Légion d'Honneur, the same ones who had come to Claire's engagement party, clapped him bravely on the shoulder, saying 'We're with you, Jérôme.'

And Papa grew younger. The crowd thinned out, and in the shade of the cypresses Mother went up to Aunt Rebecca's still figure.

'Rebecca, I thank you publicly for all the affection which my dear Claire was able to find with you.'

Aunt Rebecca didn't answer, she turned her face to the tree, she took off her black toque, she ran her fingers through her hair, and said at last:

'I don't know how you can stand these agonizing sessions.'

And then she stiffened imperceptibly, her eyes widened, she almost ran to meet a man who was coming down the path. A man such as we had never seen, a big baboon with big shoulders, big ears, big black glasses and a brown skin, like an Inca.

'Frédéric!' Aunt Rebecca cried.

'Who on earth is that?' asked Valérie, putting up her hand to shade her eyes.

Aunt Rebecca uncoiled against him, slept on his shoulder

for a moment, and then pushed him away. But the man didn't move; perhaps his black glasses made him think he was invisible.

'I'm done for, done for,' Grandma moaned.

Mother took her arm to help her up, she called to Papa: 'Help me, Jérôme. Darling Granny isn't well, these emotions aren't for someone her age.'

I keep an eye on Grandmother Cartet all the time, she never does die. She breaks one leg, then the other, she bruises her shoulder, she eats a bad oyster, she stops her heart beating by pressing on it with both hands and she falls backwards, but the moment always comes when she flutters her eyelids and asks for her glasses.

'For someone who's got her eye on Paradise, she doesn't half hang on,' says Henriette.

Grandma can't take us in; she says:

'But where do all these children come from?'

Claire in particular makes her uneasy.

'The seductive way she sticks her bottom out, my poor Véronique. But you'll have the Devil lurking under her skirts if you don't keep her in order.'

Mother gets nervous. 'You really think so?'

And the three of them, Mother, Grandma and the Canon, put their heads together and decide to break Claire in as they would a horse by sending her to the prairies of Switzerland, Germany or England.

'Where she will at least learn languages and get some fresh air without too much risk of monkey-tricks,' Grandma says.

And I picture great apes who run leaping after Claire, but Claire is not afraid. Her blood pounding, she calms them with her hand, caressing their necks; she says to them:

'From tomorrow we'll go walking together every day. I'll go first, but I'll keep turning round to look at you, to make sure the treasure you represent is still there.'

And then one of the great apes becomes Claire's favourite, he puts his front paws on her shoulders and he licks her so gently that Claire smiles, closing her eyes, and commands:

'Again and again, until the end of the world, if you want to.'

That's how I think of Claire now and often. I discover the smiles she didn't have for us. I wait to enter her settings and to find that I too am in the country of the baboons. Then, Grandma will lower her eyelids on her faded pictures, and Mother will hear from Papa's own lips how Lulu Diamant died because she wasn't allowed to have a wart on her finger.

Mother doesn't know about Lulu Diamant. We never mention her to Mother, not even when we whisper urgently that we have a secret, so that she will stay longer by our beds at night.

Charles asks her to marry him almost every night, this always goes down well with Mother, he tries to kiss her on the lips:

'I'd marry you if you weren't old.'

Mother half laughs, she wipes her lips, she holds him close, she promises to be eighteen tomorrow morning.

'Even in the bus?' asks Charles.

'Everywhere where I'm holding your hand,' Mother says.

I wait for her, my eyes wide open in the blackness. She comes, she is bigger in the dark, she strokes my forehead.

'And what's your big secret?'

And at once my secret vanishes, I only remember the time she bit me. I was small, so she knelt down to be on my level, she took my arm, she closed her teeth on it, slowly, her hot blue eyes drowning my head; she said:

'You see the effect it has?'

Because I had bitten Olivier. Afterwards I went and hid in the wardrobe and Mother's hot blue eyes continued to drown me in the darkness and I was afraid because I had discovered the wickedness deep within her.

When Claire is in the bed next to mine I am not afraid. The light is red: Claire, her thighs bare, is reading Nietzsche and biting her finger-nail. In her other hand she has a Cronin or a Gilbert Cesbron ready open so that she can switch quickly if she hears Mother's step. Mother gives a searching look like a Customs officer, she looks particularly hard at Claire, and Claire begins to smile at Mother, which means, 'I love you, I love you', but Claire doesn't dare say it and she goes and writes it down on a bit of paper which she hides under Mother's pillow. We know, because every time Mother gets in a rage with Claire, she says:

'A lot of good it is putting love-letters under my pillow.'

Papa puts on an unhappy look and Claire rushes into his arms. Papa shelters Claire against him, he wipes her tears without a word. Claire ends up by smiling, she says to Papa:

'I forgive you, I know very well it's not your fault.'

And off she goes to Switzerland, England or Germany, wherever Mother can find a family who will keep her shut up in the evenings.

Claire always comes back some night or other. She has some new skis or a list of English swear words in her pocket.

She cannot keep her face straight, she has been sent packing.

Last year she spent the whole winter with Aunt Rebecca in Nice without anyone knowing. She had escaped from her German family and she worked in films.

'Phew!' Aunt Rebecca said to Mother quite openly, 'and you aren't half lucky she's come back, my dear.'

Mother made a pretence of being broken-hearted and Claire began to smash all the vases and plates she could find, and she sobbed:

'All right, the harm's done now, I haven't got your blasted virginity any longer.'

And then, at Easter, Alain appeared. He looked at Claire and Claire went quiet. Mother made quite a thing of it.

'Alain is everything Claire needs,' she said, 'he'll know how to break her in.'

But Aunt Rebecca slipped into Papa's study and put her mauve finger-nails on his waistcoat.

'Jérôme, how can you let such a thing happen? You might as well mate fire with water.'

'What do you expect?' Papa said. 'When the bill is too big to meet it's tempting to turn to a banker.'

'Have you forgotten how that episode ended?' said Aunt Rebecca.

When we got back from the cemetery, Papa did not take off his formal clothes, he did not come to the table, he walked up and down the flat, hunting, hunting everywhere for Claire's childhood drum or one of her old blouses which was doing duty as a duster in the broom cupboard.

He carried them into Claire's room and he locked himself in. He was no longer concerned with us. He didn't shave. He didn't sleep in Mother's bed, he lay face down on Claire's divan with his feet trailing on the floor and he muttered incomprehensible words to himself. From outside the door Mother entreated him.

'Jérôme, open the door, don't leave me alone, speak to me.'

But we kept very quiet so as not to disturb Pepa who was falling in love with Claire all over again. Apparently there had been a love affair between Papa and Claire which had lasted six years. Until Mother made big eyes at Claire, telling her 'Papa's busy' each time Claire clutched Papa's trousers and gazed at him adoringly, expecting compliments, a kiss. Grandma was scared that Claire was appropriating Mother's husband.

'Just think of it, Véronique, those two have no aim in life but to sleep together, what with Claire jumping into your bed on top of Jérôme, pressing herself against him in your place.'

Grandma is scared of everything. She pulls her black shawl over her knees, her hands which she can no longer open properly are like a withered lettuce, all ten fingers bunched together and turned heavenwards, and she reels off those things in the world she doesn't want us to experience.

1. Divorces
2. Revolutions
3. Political parties other than the right one
4. Idols and immoral persons, even if they are nice
5. Sitting with your legs swinging, your arms hanging loose and your mind wandering
6. Fried food and wine before the age of fifteen

7. Rude words and those in the medical dictionary
8. Reports of accidents and petty crimes.
9. Films about adultery.
10. All authors, unless they are dead and members of the Académie Française
11. Going to the moon, even when it is possible to buy tickets in travel agencies, because God created us for this earth, once and for all
12. Cancer, tuberculosis, nervous breakdowns, because these don't run in our family
13. Having a spirit of conquest, because it is this which has ruined the world.

'If everyone had stayed quiet in his little hole and done his duty as he did in 1914,' says Grandma, 'we shouldn't have one foot on the moon and the other devoured by cancers which never killed anyone in my day. What you don't know about doesn't exist.'

When Claire died Grandma set up a new prohibition: that she should never again be alive, never again be waiting on the doorstep, eager in her white dress, perched on her long thighs which Grandma couldn't bear, and no more of those smiles which invited, restrained and excited the baboons.

Grandma preferred to make Claire into a picture in which her last face, on her last bed in the clinic, floats in a cloud edged round with pious quotations, and she advised us to shut it up between the pages of our prayer-books.

'Destroy that picture, it's a false one,' Aunt Rebecca said.

She used to come and collect us every afternoon. She wasn't in mourning. She wore dresses of pistachio, cinnamon, strawberry, orange, which fluttered round her legs when there was a wind in the street. Valérie would look her up and down when she opened the door.

'You really haven't any shame.'

'Don't make me laugh,' Aunt Rebecca retorted.

It's always like that in my family. Aunt Rebecca used to take us by the hand, she took us to the Tuileries, she hired boats which we capsized by blowing into their sails. She bought red balloons and we released them on the banks of the Seine, following their route among the clouds as we hopped on the paving stones, noses in the air, until we were staggering with dizziness.

When we were tired she sat us down on rattan chairs, she tilted the blue-and-white parasol, she snapped her fingers and the waiter came; very hot in his white coat, catching at a drop of freshness at the corner of his mouth with the tip of his tongue. He held his notepad in the hollow of his palm and wrote down in it all the colours of ice-cream we wanted.

Except blue. Charles started asking for a blue one all the time and Aunt Rebecca, who was balancing her sandal on the tip of her foot, put the back of his hand against her hip and dictated to the waiter:

'One blue ice-cream, please, for this young man.'

'I'm afraid – I mean, we haven't got any today. To-morrow, without fail,' the waiter promised.

'Aren't you lucky,' Aunt Rebecca said to Charles, 'always having a blue ice-cream tomorrow?'

We watched, uncomprehendingly, her smile open up between her two lovely wrinkles.

She told us about Claire. Claire could no longer be with us

to eat ice-creams or anything, but she was certainly not in
the tomb like a little house.

'It's a horrid memory,' Aunt Rebecca said. 'Forget it.
It's only the old who give up living in order to die.'

Claire had just disappeared for a little while. She was
with Lulu Diamant who used to drink champagne from her
cupped hand. She was with Papa in the days when he was a
gay dog with a silver-mounted cane. She was with Mother
when she used to sit on her hair while eating bananas and
peas.

Now, Claire could mount a horse in the lilac-scented
early morning, go unhurriedly across the lawns where the
sprinklers put rainbows into the fans of water, zigzag after
a yellow or a white butterfly.

Claire was recovering from life, still a bit weak. She
could smoke as much as she wanted to, even if ten years
elapsed between one cigarette and the next. No one would
hurt her any more, neither in memory nor in hope. Her life
would continue silently in our midst, she would love whom
she wished, without ever being punished. She would no
longer count the years before going off.

'And you,' Aunt Rebecca said, turning to me, 'you must
stop saying it's unjust that Grandma who is old hasn't died
before Claire.'

Claire would know how to comfort us, whether by day
or night, because she would never sleep again. And at the
sound of her name she would be able to come back for a
time, relive her daily life . . .

'Ouf,' said Aunt Rebecca, 'is that enough for you three
for today?'

The sun was turning pink, becoming fresh, and we were
going back up the Champs-Elysées right between the paws

of the Arc de Triomphe. Aunt Rebecca took us home, she made us have a bath, then she took us into the drawing-room where Mother, Valérie and Alain were talking in low voices in the shade of closed shutters. Mother felt our damp heads, she scarcely saw us, red veins had broken out in her eyes.

While waiting for Papa to emerge from Claire's room we ate instant mashed potato. Night after night Olivier, Charles and I had instant mashed potato in the old dish on which two chickens were perched to serve as handles. Mother arranged cold meat and gherkins for Alain and Valérie.

'Eat up quickly and off to bed,' she said.

We watched Mother while we traced patterns with the fork in that filthy mashed potato. Since Claire's death Mother was always too hot. Her chin glistened, she was sticky when she kissed us. She began a dozen times on her plate of cold meat, she washed her hands at the sink, she never stopped washing her hands, and then she sniffed at them.

'I can't get rid of that scent of lilies, it's as if it's got into my pores.'

We began to be aware of the great golden-hearted lilies which had been in the jam-jar beside Claire's bed; we could no longer swallow.

'Never mind,' Mother said. 'I'm not going to force you any more, I shan't make you cry any more. I'm not going to forbid you anything and you'll be happy, won't you? You won't be able to say that I've been too harsh, too strict with you.'

Alain and Valérie came into the kitchen.

'We've come to give you a hand, Mama,' Valérie announced.

She got two cans of beer out of the refrigerator, Alain pierced the tops, they drank and it left them with moustaches.

They opened the window, and outside was the Japanese acacia, the sound of the concierge's radio, the news. Alain sat on the edge of the sink, he smoked and then sprinkled his cigarette with cold water. Valérie perched on the table beside us, she hitched up her new dress with black and white stripes, she had made up her eyes lightly and well. She gazed at Alain.

'They're so sweet when they eat with their fingers.'

Idiot! We weren't eating with our fingers. Alain pretended to believe it, lightly touching the black crape in his lapel which he wore in mourning for Claire.

And then Papa emerged swearing from Claire's room. He thumped the furniture in the hall, he switched on the lights, we came running barefoot, still asleep, we found him tearing off his collar and his pearl-grey tie.

'But there isn't a single wasps' nest in Paris,' Mother was saying, buttoning her lacy housecoat the wrong way.

And Papa shook his big unshaven face. 'For God's sake, help me! I can't stand these rags another minute.'

And we actually had permission to make a noise, we shouted and laughed, we tore at his coat tails, his waistcoat, the material gave with a rending sound. Mother began to smile, her hand over her mouth, and we were so happy once again that we could have roasted Papa and hung him alive from a window to show people that he had come back. When Papa was almost stripped naked, his beautiful suit that he had put on for Claire for ever unwearable, we saw that it was not wasp stings that were causing him such distress but boils. Forty-eight boils.

At first we did not really know what it was, but we got very skilful. The tweezers, boiling water and compresses – that was me; Olivier handed the ointment, Charles stuck on the sticking-plaster. Mother superintended, sitting beside Papa while he went 'Ouch!' to please us. You could see she was glad Papa had got all those boils. Afterwards, it was even better, because Mother got them too..

Apparently this was the cue for us to leave for Brittany to stay with Alain.

'The farther apart, the closer we are,' Alain whispered when he passed us in the corridors.

Filthy beast, I said to him mentally.

But I don't know why. He went ahead with Valérie to air the house. We followed them in the night, all along the Loire where the moon floated beneath the water and the clouds which moved like giants who might slowly open their jaws to yawn. We were asleep by the end of the Loire.

It was Mother who wanted to travel by night. She prefers to drive at night now. She says Papa won't be able to recognize the Chevrolet which killed Claire.

We arrived in the very early hours of the morning. Alain's house was blue in the wind and Papa carried us in his arms and put us to bed, kissing us just as before with his prickly moustache.

We woke up with cold feet. Mother bought us seaman's jerseys – and every morning you could see a heart-shape of sunlight cut out of the shutters and we had breakfast out of cups with Gaston, Lydia and Albert written on them.

Afterwards, we were busy with Mother and Father who

had become our children. We woke them up with the tray of dressings for the boils: 'Be good, darlings, we're going to clean you up.'

Mother laughed at Father through her eyelashes. Father gave her a tiny kiss on the nose, they never left each other, they walked about holding hands. The wind flattened the tufts of Mother's hair, Father knotted a silk cravat round his neck to soothe his boils and they went to the village to get their penicillin injections. They came back with the news-papers, they stretched out on the beach against the break-water, out of the wind. The pages blew away one by one, Mother let herself lean back, she closed her eyes, Father took her hand and held it very tight and we knew that Claire had come back among us.

So we chased Claire away with loud shouts. Charles beat on his bucket, Olivier brought back a crab between his fingers.

'It pinched me, Mama,' he wailed.

'Come here,' Mother said to me, 'what's the matter with you, you're very pale, you're eating too many french fries.'

It was true, Mother no longer forbade us anything, so where french fries were concerned we made the most of it. But it was impossible not to see Claire. She was wear-ing a bathing suit which had two quarters orange, she dipped the tip of her toe into the water, she wrinkled her nose:

'Brr-rr, but it's cold, it's inhuman!'

Or else she was in the dunes with the boys who were galloping on long-maned ponies, she was recognizable by her long tawny hair, she turned round and the wind filled her mouth.

Claire was constantly the girl in the distance, the one

with the long hair who runs fast and laughs over her
shoulder.

Luckily she was not with Alain. Not at all. Alain took
part in tennis tournaments, he came back at sundown with
a navy-blue sweater knotted by the sleeves round his
shoulders; he asked from far off if we had everything we
wanted.

Each day he had more freckles on his nose, more blond
hairs on his legs. Valérie trotted behind him, she swung her
racquet, she wore pleated mini-skirts. Alain sent balls to
her against the garage door, she leapt aside and the balls
went through as if her racquet had a hole in it; she flushed.

'It's because they're watching me,' she complained. 'Buzz
off, kids.'

But we were having too much fun calling out 'Fault!'
every time without her daring to get mad at us in front of
Alain.

When our parents' boils were beginning to get better,
Alain's Henriette came and squatted on the kitchen step, a
copper pan in the hollow of her black apron. She rubbed it
for a long time with damp sand. From a distance, she
beckoned to us with her old finger.

'My treasures, you mustn't say anything more to your
parents about your sister, so that they can finally begin
getting a grip on themselves.'

Mother brought back armfuls of broom for the copper
pan, she stood back and half closed her eyes to study the
effect.

'Keep an eye on your brothers to make sure they don't
mention Claire in front of your father, it could cause us to
have a relapse.'

Papa wandered about the garden, he had resorted to his old trick of crossing his hands behind his back and picking his nails. He watched the white-sailed boats fuse into a cluster around the buoys. I crept up on him and slid an arm about his waist; he came to.

'Oh, it's you, pet. Listen, while I think of it, don't talk about Claire any more in front of your mother, she's still too much upset.'

There was nothing you could talk about any more. Except whether the scientists would discover clouds of formaldehyde in the Milky Way, ammonia near the nebula of Sagittarius.

'This indicates that it is very possible life may be the result of a sort of chemical evolution,' Papa read out.

'How fascinating!' Mother exclaimed, promptly removing the newspaper from Papa's hands.

It was necessary to play at having forgotten all the time. Alain and Valérie took part in the regatta, they came back out of breath, their legs soaked well above their yellow oilskins. A bit uneasy at having enjoyed themselves so much, they told us how tired they were.

Alain came to bring me chocolates during the siesta, I turned to face the wall without answering.

'You're wrong,' he whispered, putting on a brave voice all for me.

For this we had been created: so that we should disappear some day or other, be borne away, swallowed up, scattered by time. So that nothing remained of us but scraps of signs, worn dates. God wanted us to be alive, eating chocolate if we felt like it, going through the motions day after day as if nothing had happened, and so on and so forth, I know all that by heart.

I said 'OK' to Alain for the sake of peace.

I was lying face downwards on the lawn, wrapped in a rug, my cheeks in the grass, my nose against the earth. I was trying to recall her voice, and her eyes, and her teeth.

I was trying to tell myself about Claire as if she was a play, and how she would have arrived here with Alain, how their car would have made the tires squeal in turning. I was trying to tell myself how they would have drunk wines that sent bubbles up to your head, gone swimming in a dark blue sea. They would have talked of children, children who grow up, and they would have hollowed out their bed deep in the big white sofa that was made for Claire.

And then I raised my head, I knew that these fancies were false, that Claire could not live at Alain's side. For she talks of it at night when she thinks I'm asleep, but it isn't Alain whom she calls.

Something was out of joint in this landscape, the sea was grey, pebble-whipped, Alain's Henriette made us have boiling footbaths. There was a metronome somewhere, somewhere among the house with the blue roof, the hoary pines or the maples, the rocky reef and its hewn steps which led down to the beach where strangers had no right to come.

At dinner, Mother, Father, Valérie and Alain chatted pleasantly about the next tide, rolling rye pancakes in a layer of brown sugar, licking a last crumb off their chins. I stared at them, especially Papa who had been in love with Claire for six years and then for two days, shut up in her room, and they didn't blench. The metronome was ticking.

'Another pancake?'

'Some more cider, Mama?'

'A fine night, the sea's quiet.'

'And tomorrow we'll go and visit the oyster-beds, you eat them alive.'

'With a knife. They're lovely.'

A fine night, the sea quiet, and I was biting my pillow in the darkness, I was calling to Claire, I was squeezing my eyes as tight shut as I could.

'Come, Claire, come.'

But she didn't want to return. Night after night I was forgetting her nose, her mouth, the oval of her face, her look. When I recaptured one of her features, it was her walk, her laugh which disappeared. I got mixed up with the girls I had seen from a distance during the day, the one who galloped in the dunes with the boys, or the one who had cried out, 'Brr-rr, but it's cold, it's inhuman,' as she tested the sea with the tip of her toe. I got up and walked about in the darkness. I was no longer afraid that God might grab me by the ankles.

I said to Him: 'Rotten God!'

The metronome vibrated continually in the air, penetrated the ears, took over the whole body, making the heart beat to an oppressive cadence. I don't understand anything about their death. At boarding-school they made us say how we would spend the last five minutes of our life. Caroline copied St Louis Gonzaga; she wrote: 'I should go on playing quietly.' She was top. I put: 'If it was absolutely certain, I should throw myself out of the window so as not to wait.' I got nought, plus a report to Mother on my lack of discipline.

Every day at four o'clock we had to eat slices of bread and jam on which the sand gritted between our teeth, see Mother and Father drinking tea, which they loathe, with Alain under the parasol stuck in the lawn, watch Valérie reading her horoscope hidden between the pages of a book on philosophy, which bores her.

Life applied, life imposed, all of us caught in a fly-trap, withdrawn from the surface of the earth. Olivier and Charles were chasing each other with revolver shots under the trees; they were shouting:

'Don't move, you're dead, you're not allowed to move any more.'

My hands burrowed into the sand, bringing to light objects forgotten for weeks, orange peel, ice-cream sticks, a piece of toothless comb, and even a sandal completely worn away.

In the depths of this abandoned world larvae were ceaselessly being born, clusters of eggs were fermenting, threatening, nibbling, transporting Claire far away, ever farther, because no one wanted to speak of her any more.

Farther away than Grandpa No. 1 dressed in white in the garden of our childhood, farther away than our young grandmother who had disintegrated among the folds of her blue gown.

Far away towards a final death where only silence falls, like flakes of snow. The sun made white holes in the clouds, withdrew indefinitely to the depths of space.

I said to Claire: 'Don't worry, I won't let them do it.'

The dead don't come into kitchens, they don't go up to the metal tap which gently fills a big glass with water.

They don't stroll along the roof, spreading their arms wide like wings. They don't walk quickly along the kerb in gold Italian sandals, tossing their tawny hair. I shut my eyes and I saw Claire coming from afar, face, hands, legs like mine later on when I am grown up, and she passed through me just like that, quite easily, without colliding.

And then one morning the metronome stopped. They were simply forced to talk of her, my father in slate-grey jeans, my mother in a lemon-yellow knitted dress which buttoned down the front, Alain all blond in a white roll-necked sweater, Valérie with artificial freckles chalked on her re-modelled nose and her new wide-open eyes. Yes, everything had been thought of for breakfast: tea, ordinary coffee, decaffeinated coffee, and five sorts of jam. Yes, everything was perfectly in order, every morning before they sat down I saw the satisfaction in their eyes as they glanced around them and it always made me want to laugh. I always said to myself: They're riding for a fall, they're so pleased with themselves for being well regulated. Alain's Henriette brought it in on a plate and she said, lowering her head:

'Who am I to give it to, please?'

And we knew that Claire had received a letter. No one answered. Mother, her cheeks scarlet, poured coffee on the table, in the saucers, and even into the cups.

'It was bound to happen,' Papa said.

The letter had been placed in front of Alain. He pushed it towards Mother and Mother pushed it away a little and the letter remained in the middle of the poppy-embroidered tablecloth. There was time to see everything: the grubby envelope, obliterated, scribbled with three different ad-dresses – Paris, our house in the country, and now Alain's Brittany; the red and green stamps and the greasy purple cancellation, *Correos del Peru*, and then a lama drawn on a

mountain, BP. Perm. No. 41. And then a postmark:
Lima-Prudencia, 5 de Julio.

'Cor-reos del Pe-ru,' Valérie brayed slowly, with the
same vexed expression as if Claire had been there.

I said: 'All right, all right, there's no law against it.'

Papa took the letter, he turned it over, he deciphered the
French postmark on the back, *Paris Distribution 13 July*, he
read the words aloud haltingly, his hand began to twitch the
letter imperceptibly, then more violently.

'Jérôme,' Mother called.

As if Papa were far away, as if he had gone into exile on
the morning of July 13, that morning when Claire had gone
off without saying goodbye or anything.

'It's a very sad coincidence,' Alain said.

Sitting motionless in the wicker chair facing the window,
he was looking rather put out.

Valérie shrugged her shoulders. 'What are we going to
do?'

Mother was wide-eyed again, as when she said, 'I want
to see my child naked one last time.'

And I went very red. 'Burn it, Mama, please, please, you
mustn't open it, she wouldn't want you to, I don't want you
to.'

'We have a right to know,' Valérie said.

I looked hard at her remodelled nose. 'You want it
opened because no one's ever going to write to you from
Peru.'

Mother called me naughty in a discouraged way.

'Hasn't Claire's death taught you a lesson? Think how
remorseful you would feel if Valérie died after you had
spoken to her like that.'

I didn't want to answer. Mother slit open Claire's letter

with a knife, she took out a sheet of squared paper, not notepaper, a sheet which had been torn from a working block for a hasty note to Claire. At the last moment she said:

'I can't. Read it aloud, Alain.'

'No,' Alain said, 'I'd rather Father did.'

'Very well,' Papa said, 'we'll do it as in the song: the smallest one shall be eaten first. You there, come along.'

I couldn't believe it but Papa was smiling out of the corner of his eye, as he must have smiled at Lulu Diamant, as he used to smile at Claire when he was putting on his pearl-grey tie to take her out to eat oysters. This was the father I adored. I climbed on his knee, and the sun came out from behind a cloud, lit up the table and retired again at once. Papa had unfolded the sheet. I cleared my throat.

'Shall I start, Papa?'

He signalled yes, with his little smile. Perhaps he had read the beginning. It was a difficult handwriting, so I had to go slowly.

Iquitos, July 5.

My little doe,

Ninety degrees in the shade. Not much sleep, lots of work. Indolent people – impossible to make them get a move on because of the heat. Heavy rains which turn everything into a swamp. Endless difficulties . . . please turn over . . .

. . . and yet I manage to worry about you.

What are you doing? What's happening to you? I want so much to know that you are happy. One way or another, my life is settled. I am eager for you to see what I'm shooting at present. I am full of plans for both of us. A Canadian

TV series and an Italian documentary on motor-racing, you'll see. I'll tell you all about it. Think of me very hard, I'll sense it and I'll have the feeling you are writing to me.

I shall be back on July 12 or 13, perhaps before this letter reaches you; the post is erratic here. I'll send you a telegram. Here's to us! I kiss you tenderly.

Frédéric.

Valérie uttered an exclamation, she pointed to someone invisible, she said:

'Mother, it's him. The man who came to the funeral, Aunt Rebecca kissed him, she would, she's never had any morals. And he's in films, what's more, not that that surprises me with those dark glasses.'

Was that big baboon with dark glasses the man who sent the blue telegram, who had the rendezvous in the Pole Star? I said to Claire: 'Well! Who'd have thought it!' just as she had said because I had grown up so much. 'So someone loves you all the way to Peru?'

Alain bowed his head, he was tracing lines on the table-cloth with a knife. The lines on his forehead looked as if they were drawn with a pencil. Papa folded the letter, he cleared his throat; it sounded to me as if he whinnied softly – the noise horses make when they've broken out – but I may have been mistaken. Mother was piling the toast up piece by piece on her right, and then she looked at Alain with eyes in which Claire lived again, she wanted Claire to be sorry, she said:

'Alain, can you forgive me? I was wrong, I blame myself, but at the same time it was such a joy for me . . . oh, forgive me, forgive me for having shocked you all.'

91

Papa evidently felt Mother was overdoing it.

'But, Véronique, there's no forgiveness to ask. They'd already said goodbye in secret. And kissed. And she'd even given him a photograph of herself and cautioned him not to show it to anyone, ever.'

We all looked at Papa as if he had gone mad.

'You're making it up,' Mother said hurriedly.

'No, no,' Papa said, 'when you love it's for life.'

He put on a knowing air, he cleared his throat several times to get rid of his embarrassment, and then he said:

'That's enough. It's too awful, and of no interest anyway.'

He made me get down off his knee and he went out without looking at anyone.

'My little doe!' Valérie repeated. 'He calls her "my little doe" in front of us!'

She gave a sort of snigger. I was watching a fly wash his feet in the jam and I wanted to smile. In my mind's eye was a tall man with dark glasses, his hands in his pockets, he was whistling the song of the cowboy who is going to eat a roast chicken.

A tousled Claire was dreaming in the sun, exposing her small nose to the sun, finding life good in the sun, and it was just too bad if from now on her eyes were blank.

That was it, the life I wanted, beyond the limits of the metronome, passing at one bound from Peru to the too-well-run house in Brittany, unafraid of the earth which swallows you up because the earth is so vast.

Unafraid of lances, arrows, wildfire, bombs, all those sufferings in the dictionary. Unafraid of revolutions, cancer, trips to the moon, all those prohibitions of Grandma's. Without going down on your knees, without taking tea, without wanting a first-class moral situation.

And I looked at Claire without seeing her, Claire tearing the blue telegram into tiny pieces with her teeth, eating it, to make sure she didn't forget and leave it behind her when she went off.

Mother took the letter back, she turned it over between her fingers.

'It's just to read it one last time. Afterwards, that's that ... all the same, I shouldn't like Claire's memory to be tarnished.'

'That would certainly be regrettable,' Alain murmured.

I stood up, I was at least eighteen, and I said to Mother as one equal to another:

'I don't see who you want to be so considerate of. In any case, Alain can no longer break off his engagement to Claire.'

Mother cut me down to size at top speed, she gave me a slap.

Mother and I fought a duel. I put on my Peruvian shirt with the lace cuffs, my black trousers with a wide belt, my boots with silver spurs, I lifted the safety-catch and cocked my pistols, and after the slap I aimed straight at Mother.

'Do you really want to make me go off, like Claire?'

Except for the day she bit me, Mother had never dared to touch me. When she is in a good mood she says, 'You make me nervous, looking at me like that.' When she is over-wrought, she says, 'Stop looking at me like that.'

That's all. She has never yet dared to lift a finger against me. Against Claire, yes, all the time. Henriette says: 'If you reckoned up all the slaps your mother's given that child, you'd have enough for a round of applause lasting five minutes.'

'Go to your room,' Mother got out. 'Go on, you don't know what you're saying.'

Alain and Valérie hadn't moved, I saw their eyes like little balls of feathers ready to utter shrill cries. I said to Mother:

'All right, you come too, I want to talk to you.'

We went upstairs in single file, straight into the Peruvian desert, with a threat in every cactus and the illusion that perhaps everything might yet become pure, easy, that once over the horizon, you could if need be forget everything.

You could see silhouettes coming a long way off and choose which to encounter, which to avoid. In my room Mother leaned against the door, very pale, buckling a bit at the knees; I said to her:

'Why did you always shut her up, slap her, punish her . . . Why?'

'It was necessary,' Mother moaned, 'you're making me ill, be quiet, darling, you can't understand.'

She hid her face and I heard myself cry out:

'Why? Tell me what she did to you.'

'She was stubborn, she didn't want to obey, she would have done herself some mischief, you can't understand,' Mother repeated.

Mother and I faced each other. The silence was so intense that I thought I heard it fall, shatter with tiny, violent explosions at our feet. My heart leapt in front of me, red, shapeless, striated as in an anatomy illustration, and it beat with the flapping sound of damp valves.

I said to Mother:

'She cried, she used to cry very quietly at night and say, "What does it all mean, Frédéric? Are you thinking of me? Do you sometimes think I'm the only one for you?"'

'Ah, I thought as much,' Mother said, letting herself sink down on the bed.

She had that look which she has acquired since Claire's death, a bit distraught with helpless sorrow; she begged gently:

'Go on, darling.'

'She talked of other things too, and she laughed very loudly, and I was afraid she'd know I'd wakened up.'

'More,' Mother demanded.

But I couldn't tell her about Claire. I took off my silver-spurred boots and my pistols, and I went and sat beside Mother.

'You can punish me, if you like,' I said to comfort her.

'Never again,' Mother said.

And she took me in her arms and stroked my hair, murmuring to herself and pretending to sleep, her eyes closed:

'Go to sleep, my joy, my little treasure, Mama's going to make it all better.'

The words she says when we are sick and we go to sleep with her hand hugged against our hearts. In order to think of Claire while in Mother's arms, I had to shut my eyes and I couldn't bear any more.

I keep hearing Claire on that last night when she whirled round and round like a white flame, when she stopped in front of me:

'Swear you won't say anything?'

I didn't answer. I pretended to be sleepy and I pulled the sheet up over my head and said my prayer that makes me drop off: 'Please, God, forget all about me.' But I couldn't go to sleep, Claire began to cry very quietly in the darkness, and to laugh very loudly, and she murmured: 'I need you very often, I call you. I imagine I'm unhappy because you aren't there. I say, "My Frédéric, my Frédéric," I say it over and over again, and at other times I think of killing myself. I think of dying. Because I tell myself I've had all I'm going to get out of life.

'I should like to stop living,' Claire said that night in that stifled voice which carries so far when you want very much to cry. 'Not really stop living, because there's always hope. I still have hope; I very often say to myself, "It isn't possible that . . . that one day I shan't be living with Frédéric." I should have liked to have your child, I should have liked to have last year's little child, to dream of a child growing up, sleeping between us on the big white sofa. It would be born by now. You didn't want that. You said you were scared of me. Because I wanted to make you believe I was all alone.

'That I had no family at the back of me. That I had no allowance at the back of me. That I had nothing at the back of me.

'I no longer know what I want. I no longer know what I'm waiting for. I'm waiting for tomorrow. One last time tomorrow. Afterwards, only meetings with you in the Pole Star? Ridiculous. And afterwards? Nothing. And afterwards, it's so long. To have courage . . . to put up with Alain kissing me whenever he feels like it. It's hard. I don't know where we are any longer.'

And then Claire began to laugh in the darkness, she squatted on her bed in her white nightgown like bedouins watching for the dawn. She laughed wildly:

'People who love me say I'm not mature. I love myself,

and I too tell myself I'm not mature but that I may as well resign myself to it, because at my age . . . Often I can't help laughing. Everything is so stupid. My days have become so empty. I have very little cause for pride when it comes to taking a long, hard look at myself. Still . . . if I must remember . . . to have had an abortion . . . to have kidded myself – what? – two hundred times?'

And then Claire lay down again in the dark, she put on a worldly tone as if she were really talking to someone:

'Now Frédéric, please don't look like that, you know quite well my feelings towards you haven't changed. Yes, yes, I know you love me. In your fashion! You say, "We'll never be separated." From time to time you start again; you say: "It's like being half of twins." You say of us, "We *are* twins." And when you're depressed you say, "Thank heavens you're there!" Or else, with a deep sigh, "Just so long as one of us doesn't go away."

'If I have a child that isn't yours, I feel as if this stranger will destroy me. But wouldn't it be perfectly possible for an idiot like me not to love you, deep down? For me to be acting out one of your films? Since I can't live with you, I've got to pretend to myself that I love you. Isn't that smart?

'If only one could know instead of imagining. For a long time you believe love is – well, powerful emotions. Need for Frédéric. Frédéric the one and only. Eye of my being. Now, I believe love, or so-called love, is a kinship. You can't deny your father or your mother. You're stuck with them for life, whether they suit you or not. So when you love someone, when you love Frédéric, you can feel anguish, or the desire to hurt him, to avenge yourself, you can even make a foolish

marriage with someone else, like I'm going to do, yet in spite
of everything he's a part of you and that's that.'

'You're a part of me and that's all there is to it,' Claire said
to the absent Frédéric. 'Do you know what even Gaspard
said? He said, "Frédéric's marriage will never work." He
said your wife was bossy. You'd be furious, wouldn't you,
if you knew? He said you look unhappy. He said you and I
had spoilt something. You said as much yourself. You said
it in your car going down the Avenue d'Iéna one evening,
and I said to you, "No, no, you mustn't kiss me, now that
I'm going to be married someone might see us."
      'I'm waiting for you to write to me. You always say,
"I'll write you as soon as I get there." Every time you're far
away I miss you and you write to me and I tear up the letter
or the postcard or the telegram. Because I'm afraid someone
might find it. It's a pity I have such a good memory. You
can't help wondering why.
      'Why? It's incomprehensible. When I told you that I too
was going to get married, you gave me the little chain. It
went all black round my neck. So I said to myself, it's
because our love has gone all black and can't be shown in
daylight that the little chain has blackened.
      'You told me that you were both delighted and desolated
by my marriage. So far as being delighted is concerned, I
hope you lied.
      'And when you went off and got married, you telephoned
me, you were speaking very quietly, you were afraid she'd
hear you, and you told me that . . .

'. . . That you were very frightened,' Claire repeated,
choking. 'That you carried on you the little good-luck

charm I'd given you. Frédéric, it's not true, is it? The whole thing's impossible. A hateful trick. I don't understand.'

She sniffed two or three times and then she adopted a new, reasonable tone:

'You ought to be happy. That's what I tell myself, but it doesn't make me glad. I mean, yes, it does make me glad but it's no consolation. Frédéric, I was happy with you. Not so much happy as thinking I was happy. Deep down, yes, it would be better for you to be really happy with your wife, it *is* better, and I hope . . .

'I hope the pair of you will have a child, and all. What's the sense? I can't understand. I can't understand any longer. And day after day goes by and nothing gets sorted out.

'I think that one day, in spite of everything . . . in spite of everything, I'm afraid . . . afraid I'm going to kill myself. That will mean denying myself all the . . . all the things that can still happen. But perhaps I haven't enough imagination, I don't see what else is going to happen to me . . . I don't see any more. I don't wish for anything to happen to me any more. Apart from tomorrow. To hear you, to talk to you. To imagine that everything's going to be rubbed out and begin again.'

And then she went to sleep. Or I did. The next morning she didn't want to waken me. She didn't say goodbye or anything. She went away and she is dead. So inevitably I know it all by heart.

Papa too is a traitor. I was so ashamed of having thought of Claire while in Mother's arms, so ashamed that she didn't want to punish me when I said, 'Do you really want to make me go off, like Claire?' that I went and hid in the car.

I'm very good at hiding-places. They never look in

cupboards or in the car, they never think of it, they always call in distant places where you aren't.

I wanted to stay in the car for ever, until they forgot about me and they went back to Paris with me all dried up and my jaw-bone placed on the back seat, but I was so hungry that this eventuality got too complicated. When I was sure they had gone to bed, I uncurled from under the pull-down seats and emerged. My legs were as tottery as a lamb's, and I had noises in my ears. I didn't quite know what to do, I walked to the corner of the garage, the house was in darkness.

And I saw Papa, stock still, close by. And I thought that Papa was huge, that he had warm arms in which you could be carried, and I found myself up there in his arms. For once, my trick of curling my toes tight inside my shoes didn't work, I couldn't help sniffing, but I wasn't too ashamed because Papa shot the bolt on the kitchen door and promised that no one would see me.

We ate fried eggs and eleven slices of bread dunked in chocolate made with milk. Papa took me on his knee, he wanted to know why I had disappeared. He said 'disappeared' as people say about Claire, and then it came out in spite of me and I said:

'Because I don't want to live with you any longer.'

'Why?' Papa asked.

'Because I don't want to get like you.'

'Just what do you think is so dreadful about us?'

I could tell from Papa's voice that he wasn't taking me seriously, so it was even more difficult to explain.

'I don't know. The metronome. Grandma. The Canon. Being forbidden to go to the moon even when everybody's going. The lot.'

'The metronome?' Papa queried, smiling under his moustache.

'That thing . . . that thing that makes you do everything.'

'Right,' said Papa. 'Let's try to be a bit more specific. What exactly is it you *do* want, do you know?'

'I want to be like Claire. Like Lulu Diamant.'

'Lulu Diamant? Who's been talking to you about her?'

'Aunt Rebecca.'

Papa put me down on the ground; he crossed his legs and said:

'Your dear aunt's a bit haywire, you know.'

He said that Lulu Diamant was named Madeleine Trignon. She came from Brittany, but she spoke with an English accent. She used to say that her dream was to watch rain falling from behind the windows of a hut while eating chestnuts dipped in fresh cream with her fingers. She was lying, she didn't want to eat. One of her aims in life was to have ribs like the bars of a cage in which her heart fluttered.

'Put your hand there, Jérôme, feel how close it is, you could almost take it with a twist of your wrist, as a fisherman reels in his line; do you want to?'

Papa used to go and wait for her outside the mannequins' exit in the Rue Royale, and that was quite a sight! These clever young ladies in all their grace, walking affectedly, parading jewellery and good fortune . . .

Some had had political or diplomatic careers. You could still recognize some of them on the front pages of the news-papers, they had not lost the carriage of their heads, their mysterious mouths, their silence.

But Lulu Diamant couldn't bear silence, she hurried to Maxim's, she fed on champagne.

'You see, Jérôme, it's chemical, we are what we eat, I shall end up by becoming bubbles, froth, foam in the sunlight.'

Lulu Diamant was unreasonable. Papa was dropping with sleep, she prevented him from closing his eyes.

'If you cease looking at me for an instant I shall cease to exist, I feel it, I feel it.'

Papa had begun to be aware of an itching all over his body, it was Lulu Diamant who was nibbling at him bit by bit.

'Like the outbreak of boils after Claire died?'

Papa didn't answer me. Lulu Diamant wanted him all for herself, she had admitted it, closing her eyes and smiling gently:

'Day after day, until the end of the world, if you want to.'

Papa had taken fright, Lulu Diamant was already vanishing in bubbles, you could see it in her ever more brilliant gaze, her ever more transparent chest where her heart was fluttering ever more wildly.

Grandpa No. 1 was angry.

'Look here, Jérôme, you're not going to land yourself with an invalid, are you? A girl who comes from nowhere will get nowhere, believe me. A girl who has neither family nor allowance at the back of her. Who has nothing at the back of her.'

Papa had believed Grandpa. He had told Lulu Diamant politely that he was going to think things over. Lulu Diamant had understood. She had smiled at Papa, her lipstick put on askew for the only time in her life.

The two of them had said goodbye in secret. They had kissed, and she had even given him a photograph of herself, cautioning him not to show it to anyone, ever.

She had promptly married a banker. She had not become any less unreasonable, she continued refusing to eat,
her stomach became so small that a biscuit was enough to
fill it.

'In actual fact,' Papa said, 'poor dear Madeleine wasn't
over bright.'

I heard Papa out to the end. I made my fingers move
one after the other, thumb, index, middle finger, ring
finger, thumb again. I didn't remind Papa of the wart Lulu
Diamant used to have on her finger, he had forgotten too
much.

I looked at him, his face tired, almost puffy, greying, the
remains of a boil under his chin. I said to him:

'You know, I love you very much, all the same.'

There was a forgiveness session with Mother. She said as
usual:

'I forgive you and you forgive me.'

It's her formula. You don't know what to do with yourself. There she is in front of us, and her eyes are getting ever
warmer, ever bluer; she says, laughing:

'My poor darling, you have a hopeless mother, a nervy
mother, a mother who doesn't really love you one bit.'

We just sigh. This time, I had to ask forgiveness of Alain,
Valérie, and even of Olivier and Charles because it seems
that I had transgressed against everybody by hiding in the
car. I did everything required of me.

'You see, darling, you have to make the most of the
holidays to set yourself up, put on a bit of weight if possible
so that you can get 'flu in the autumn without losing the
benefit of this good sea air.'

'Breathe deeply – ahh-h-h – that gets rid of the toxins.

Those rosy cheeks children get represent a capital investment in health which we're giving you.'

'Think of the children who never go away on holiday, and their pasty faces.'

'We've been through a very trying time, but we've won through with God's help. Besides, the worst is over.'

'Believe in the life everlasting, that helps for sure.'

'There'd be nothing to stay alive for, otherwise.'

'I'm dreading the return to Paris, when we're going to find all those things that belong to Claire. It'll be heart-breaking to pick up a dress she'll never wear again, a scarf, a scent-bottle.'

'You ought to write to Henriette and tell her to give all Claire's things to a society for helping poor girls. And then maybe have the room redecorated.'

'You're right, that's settled. But we shall all have a special memory, think carefully before I write.'

'We ought to burn the remaining invitations.'

'My living little girl who will never be forty. Am I wrong to think of her?'

'God in his goodness has spared her the sufferings, dangers, sorrows of life; that's what you've got to keep telling yourself.'

'Alain, don't think me cruel, but I do sometimes think you mightn't have been very happy with Claire. She was too young, too impulsive still.'

'I shall never forget that you were her last joy on earth, Alain. Basically, she died happy, didn't she?'

'Say it to me, darlings, say it to me, or I couldn't get over it.'

Who was it talking like this? Father, Mother, Valérie,

Alain, anyone, sitting interminably around the tea-table because it was raining.

Scents of tar, rotting seaweed, damp sand, dead leaves, drifted in. Olivier and Charles had dubbed Alain's Henriette 'Boblock'. They spent their time squabbling as to who should climb on her back. She was on hands and knees polishing the treads of the staircase.

'You see if I don't lash out just now so that you keep the mark of my five fingers on your bottoms,' she grumbled.

But they continued to flog her with the duster.

'Gee up, Boblock.'

I stepped over them to go up to my room.

'Is it true you're at the awkward age?' Charles crowed in his raucous voice. 'Mother said so while you were hidden in the car.'

I locked the door. The walls were blank. The bedspread was red-and-white checks, and so were the curtains. Sometimes there was a grasshopper on the bleached floorboards. I sat down beside it, my knees under my chin. I made a prison for it with my hand. It jumped, it tickled me, I imagined it looking for a means of escape, unmethodical but tireless. And then, for no reason, it gave up in the depths of its hole, it shammed dead. And then, once again, I felt its legs feeling round frantically in all directions, nothing deterred it, nothing halted it, as if the black hole of my closed hand had become its whole existence in the world, without hope of escape.

I uncurled my fingers, I left it an opening under my thumb, but the stupid creature didn't find it. Its grasshopper mind went on blundering around, it had already lost the memory of anywhere else. I opened my hand.

Outside, night was falling. I went down to join the others round the tea-table.

'You don't know what to do with children when it rains,' someone said.

What I like about the green classroom is that the sun shines in on me. It warms the whole of the left-hand row under the windows and during the summer term there are five girls with one arm and one cheek sun-tanned. In front of the blackboard Sister Dolly is teaching us how to make a telephone call in English. When my turn comes I go up on the platform, form an earpiece with my clenched hand, Sister Dolly does the same, and we make a long-distance call.

'How do you do?' Sister Dolly yells enthusiastically.

I too begin to shout almost, to make sure she hears.

'How is Claire?'

'She's fine,' Sister Dolly says.

'Has she eaten her rotten chicken?'

Sister Dolly cuts off the call.

'Not "rotten", dear. "Rotten" is "*pourri*".'

I always say 'rotten' for 'roast'. But we are only doing farmyard vocabulary and as yet we haven't many subjects of conversation. Sister Dolly smells of café au lait and dust, she strides when she walks, making her rosary clink in the folds of her skirt. Caroline swears she's a boy in disguise.

Caroline is my best friend. At least, she has chosen me for best friend. She looks like Bobby, our cocker spaniel, with her chestnut hair hanging down on each side of her pointed chin. To please her, I play at being as fed up as she is on those Sundays when we aren't going out and when our parents can come and visit us in the parlour. We sit on the lawn. Caroline tears out grassblades one by one, every five minutes she asks:

'You mind too, don't you, Berthe, that your parents won't be coming?'

'Yes, of course, Berthe,' I reply.

Caroline and I call each other Berthe. Our beds are next to each other in the green dormitory, and in the morning we say to each other:

'Hi, Berthe!'

'Hi, Berthe!'

That way we aren't anybody, and it's fun. During the hours of supervised recreation we walk in the grounds, except near the wall, there are bushes there and it's out of bounds. Caroline jumps as high as possible. 'You don't see anything with that wall,' she moans, 'I'd like to get out of here.'

I am quite content behind the wall. There's an old horse with a sway back wandering about who's called Cloclo, he rests his nose in the palms of our hands, he blows lengthily, an electric shiver runs up his spine and makes the flies buzz off. On the other side of the community's enclosure you can see the nuns playing ball. Girls walk slowly up and down the paths in pairs, they are whispering, they are letting their hair grow or putting it up in a new way, and a year always comes when the colour of the ribbon in our lapels changes. Pink for the little ones, green for our lot, blue for the seniors.

Changing my ribbon is the one thing that interests me, that and the old girls coming back for our feast-day. They bring a breath of the beyond, they have passed from a small world to a big one, you can see it in the way the nuns talk to them, catty and curious, even enquiring after the children they're expecting as they hide their laughter behind their hands.

I observe them as much as I can. Caroline tugs at my hand.

'Berthe, stop looking at them like that. You've got a way of staring at people, you're going to have trouble with the boys later on.'

Caroline thinks only of boys. In the train which takes us back to Paris one Saturday in four she sits where she can make eyes at the guard. She claims he makes eyes back.

When we returned in September Caroline wanted to shock me, she produced a bra she had pinched from her mother and put her hands on her hips.

'What do you bet I'm wearing it by the spring?'

'My *dear* Berthe, *I* don't need that to get hold of a boy-friend.'

Afterwards, every evening, we played at telling ourselves about Frédéric in the dark.

'Unfortunately he has to wear dark glasses, even for sleeping. He burnt his eyes while filming the sun on board a jet. At that altitude the sun fairly gobbles up your sight, you know. He came down blind, his mother was frantic with anxiety.'

Caroline pretended to be overwhelmed.

'Poor Berthe! So when you have a photograph taken of the pair of you, you're always going to look as if you're on the arm of a condemned man, because those dark glasses will make him look as if he was blindfolded to conceal his identity.'

'It'll be very practical when he's famous, remember.'

Caroline turned over in her bed with rage. She spoke with her nose in the pillow.

'What films has he made so far?'

'Oh,' I said lightly, 'he has masses of projects. He's swamped with projects, always between two planes, between Peru and Brittany. I don't think he'll have very much time to see me this year. We're getting married in four years' time.'

'Poor Berthe,' sighed Caroline, 'he'll have found someone else with sun-glasses and a bronzed skin emerging from a white bikini.'

I wasn't worried. Frédéric liked girls with long tawny hair, girls so tense that sometimes you see their hip-bones like two pebbles marking out the extent of the tiny field of their belly. Exactly like I shall be later on.

'Are you sure of it, Berthe?'

'Look, Berthe, he writes to me. He even calls me "my little doe".'

But after the first parlour Caroline came running back across the gravel, tossing her chestnut hair, calling 'Berthe! Berthe!' in a high-pitched voice through each window of the green classroom in turn.

She kicked open the door, she looked at me with her little brown eyes screwed up; she began to shriek:

'You dirty liar, Berthe! Your Frédéric's all pretend. The truth is that your sister died during the holidays, your mother wrote to my mother so that I should be nice to you. I'm blowed if I'm going to be nice to a dirty liar like you!'

And everything went silent and deathly white, with only the blows of my beating heart exploding as if they came from under ground. I looked towards the window, but there was nothing to see, only a jumbled mass. I raised my desk-lid to shelter behind it a bit and I said:

'It's absolutely untrue, Berthe, I swear it.'

Caroline leapt upon me, she shook me by the hair, yelling all the time:

'Liar, you're going to tell me the truth!'

And I grabbed her by the hair in return, I managed to bite her wrist, and she shrieked blue murder, and I called her a bitch and Sister Dolly came in.

'Her sister's dead,' panted Caroline, 'and she doesn't want to say so.'

'How horrible, poor little lamb, there, there,' said Sister Dolly.

She folded me in her arms, in her smell of café au lait and dust, and I sniffed back all the tears I was going to shed. I broke out of her arms, I looked her straight in the eye like she's always asking us to, and I said to her:

'No ... not true. My mother lost a tiny baby ... miscarriage ... there!'

'What?'

'Tiny baby,' I repeated, indicating with my hands its small dimensions. 'But she's going to have another ... honest!'

Afterwards Caroline and I were alone in the green classroom; we tried to read *Moby Dick*, sitting side by side, without speaking, without looking at each other. And then I felt that something was coming from much farther off than the decaying woods where, when you put your foot on the dead leaves, it makes a dark patch ooze out around your footprint. I saw dark spots dripping one by one on to my

knees, on to my navy-blue overall. Caroline saw them too.
She said timidly:

'Berthe, listen . . .'

I let my head sink down between my folded arms on the
desk. There was no longer anything to fight against. I said
to her:

'You did a horrid thing, Berthe. Now I want Claire to be
here.'

And I pressed my forehead against the wood of the desk,
my eyes stared into darkness, waves of sorrow-that-makes-
you-shiver ran up and down my spine, like on Cloclo's. I
flowed into the void, a well hollowed out in the depths of
the concrete desert, flowing slowly with the rest of the
universe, the green classroom, Sister Dolly, Mother, Father,
all of us no more distinguishable than the specks of mica
which glitter in the stairs on the Métro. All of us nothing
at all, and if we were really nothing at all, then Claire could
come back, there were so many thousands of years behind
us that the odds were even.

The shudders of sorrow-that-makes-you-shiver swept
over me sweetly, became a real sweetness, an ever-growing
sweetness, joy, joy everywhere. I looked up and there was
Claire.

Not visible, of course, but living down to the most forgotten reaches of my being, caught between the walls of
the green classroom, her body divided up into desks, blackboard, windows now almost dark. Present in the myriad
roll-calls that were going on around us, the whistle of the
seven o'clock train, the shrill voices of girls passing in the
corridors, the muted sound of television somewhere.

'Berthe,' Caroline said softly, 'move over, listen. We'll

have to put the light on, we aren't allowed to stay in the dark.'

'Just a minute. Listen, Berthe, I've got the knack, I can see her as much as I want.'

'Where?' Caroline asked shakily.

I leapt to my feet, I burst out laughing – 'There!' – pointing to the blackboard, the platform, everything. Caroline gave a moan.

'I'm scared stiff, Berthe. What's she like? Tell.'

I only wanted to make Caroline mad, but there was Claire wearing a low-necked yellow sweater, black flared trousers, and Italian gold sandals. Her hair flowed down over her arms, her footsteps made no sound on the gravel when she joined us on the path at the clinic the day they soldered her into the box.

'I don't understand, Berthe. I've never seen her dressed like that, can you imagine Mother allowing it!'

We switched on the light and thought about it. Caroline was biting her nails.

'Look, Berthe, if she went away from you without saying goodbye, perhaps she didn't want to come back. In such cases, you can just imagine how you make the most of it to do everything which was forbidden. If I got out of here, you can be dead sure I'd go in bashed-up cars with the guard on the train, I'd tickle his moustache, and we'd spit peanut-shells on the ground. Can you picture my mother's face if someone told her? It's the same thing.'

'How did she die?' Caroline whispered.

She wanted to talk of Claire all the time. I pulled my sheet over my head, but Caroline was leaning out of her bed, pinching me.

'Be quiet, she's taken off her veil.'

By the glow of the night-light you could see Sister Dolly's head through the dulled glass of her cubicle, round now and no longer under canvas.

The other girls were asleep, but we had to wait for Louisa, Caroline's neighbour, to thrust three fingers in her mouth and start sucking before we could be sure we were the only ones awake.

'Frédéric fired a revolver bullet through her heart,' I whispered.

'You're lying, Berthe,' Caroline said patiently.

'Look, Berthe, she's my sister, not yours.'

'Well, how?' Caroline asked again.

'She was blown up by a bomb and the gendarmes had to draw her body on the highway for her to be recognizable.'

'Too bad for you,' Caroline said. 'I'm going to get at the truth.'

I put my fingers in my ears so as to have my head full of air, I stiffened in an arc from head to heels, but I never reached that vast tract in which Claire had escaped from restraints, from orders, from permissions. Silently, I cried out as if I would never stop:

'Claire, I want to see you truly, only once, just once, come.'

I felt she was approaching, I didn't dare breathe.

'I promise I won't look, come, oh, come.'

And then the air forced its way into my lungs and the bubble burst in which Claire and I had been contained. So I rolled over to the edge of the bed to leave plenty of room for Claire in case she should come while I was sleeping.

'Are you asleep, Berthe?' Caroline whispered.

'Yes, Berthe, shut up.'

And I didn't move **again**. Short of putting a hand on my heart, no one in the whole world could have known if I was alive.

Every fourth Saturday we had to go home. The first Saturday I came home ran true to form, Mother put on a suspicious air:

'Haven't you got a note for me from Sister Dolly? Are you sure you gave her my letter?'

I pulled on my socks so that she shouldn't see my face.

'The proof that she knows, Mama, is that she's included Claire in evening prayers.'

There was a new calmness about Mother. She never stopped parting the saffron curtains a little, ranging the liqueur bottles in order of height, going to see if that was really a mark down there that Olivier, Charles and I had made on the wall, with our habit of putting our dirty paws everywhere.

Papa was old. He made 'phone calls, piled up relevant documents on his desk, went off in the car with his camera to take photographs of the inverted triangle (which means 'Stop!') at the crossing with the highway where the big Chevrolet had struck Claire. Papa talked to himself, he kept sitting down and getting up again.

'I'll have his hide. I'll have his driving licence revoked. We'll see how he gets on selling his pigs on foot. I'll have him put in prison. I'll ruin him. Thousands in damages and interest.'

He walked around with a pile of bills tucked under his arm, he put them down beside him, on his night-table before going to bed, he talked to Mr. Nobody, thumping the papers with the back of his hand:

'They're all there, from the maternity home's bill right up to the expenses we had incurred for her wedding. He's going to pay me for her wedding-dress. Maybe he thinks I'm going to let myself be dispossessed? A child represents capital, and so we shall claim.'

And then he collapsed into a chair, he began to cry, his big grey face working. Mother signalled to me silently to go and comfort him. But I passed in front of him without looking at him. I was disgusted with tears. To grow up, to get away, you have to need no one. You have to be alone in the world. Alone and at the same time everywhere. From Peru to Brittany in an instant.

I kept repeating to myself, 'That's how it is, yah, yah, yah', as I hopped on one foot down the corridor.

Everyone is wearing black for a court hearing. There are long rows of benches, like there are in the green classroom, but they are almost empty. The lawyers are lined up under the blackboard; their faces are whitened with chalk, with just a red mark for their mouths. For once, Mother and Father are thin. They stand side by side, their hands clenched on an iron bar. There is an advocate in a flowing gown who walks very fast and the hem of his gown flutters; the sleeves flutter too when he raises his hands on high and declaims:

'Ladies and gentlemen, salmon at one hundred francs a kilo. Four hundred and eighty francs for a beige hacking jacket edged with brown, to be worn over slacks. One thousand francs for a lawn with one million grassblades on which this young lady spent some time in growing up.'

Seated at a rickety table, a hairy dwarf with a straggling goatee beard that has been waxed black with boot-polish cries out as each figure is quoted:

'I make it the same.'

That's just to look impressive. He turns the handle of an adding machine to record the sum, and the ribbon of paper unwinds, coils, until it falls to the dusty floor, where it arches and squirms like a giant worm. And the dwarf turns a mighty somersault and lands neatly on his feet before the row of lawyers, and announces in a nasal voice:

'One hundred and seventy-seven thousand, eight hundred and forty hours of preparation for the death of this young lady weighing forty-six kilos ... How much per kilo do you make that, ladies and gentlemen, so that I can finish my calculations?'

'Objection!' shouts the advocate. 'The hours of sunshine are much dearer. Additional expenses must be allowed to cover the cost of strawberry ices, and all the silly magazines that go unread during the winter months. And what about the hire of the bicycle for the last journey? Aren't you going to allow me anything for that?'

Papa opens his wallet pathetically, he shakes it to show that it's empty.

'They've taken all I had,' he says brokenly. 'Look, I've got nothing left. My other children are completely worthless.'

The leading lawyer strikes a resounding blow with his gavel; he says to Papa:

'You have purchased the right to say nothing. Make the most of it. Murderer, stand forth.'

A very ordinary little man comes in. He walks on all fours, keeping his legs carefully extended to avoid bagging the knees of his new trousers, which are greeny-grey like a badly cleaned copper pan. His mouth is the only indecent thing about him: it has a cluster of white bubbles. He has a

voice like a little baboon, he shuffles on his knees towards
Mother and Father, he holds out his clasped hands towards
them:

'God the Father and God the Mother, forgive me that I
have not trespassed against you. My faith sustains me, and
so does the fender of my car, look at the experts' report, it's
hardly scratched. The sun is my witness and will confirm
my statement when I say that your daughter flung herself
upon me so that I should protect and save her. She said to
me:

' "Ah, there you are at last, monsieur. I was waiting for
you. Admittedly, your face is not very handsome; I've
known far handsomer, if you only knew the faces they've
sent me from Peru! But don't let's waste any time; you'll do
very well, none the less." '

'Not true,' Mother cries. 'We were expecting Claire for
lunch.'

The little man shakes his head sadly.

'I wouldn't lie in your presence, God the Mother. She
even insisted on paying her fare with a diamond worth
twenty-five thousand francs which she wore on the ring
finger of her left hand. Why,' he went on, 'she virtually
made the journey unaided. I'm very much afraid I was used
only as a means of transport in this business, nothing more.'

'In that case, I'll have my diamond back,' Alain says
tonelessly.

'Were *you* there?' Mother says. 'May I ask by what right
you are listening to our estimates? The courtesies are over
now, my lad. You're good for nothing but marriage. Wait
till your turn comes round. In silence, you understand?'

The dwarf with the goatee beard is getting impatient.
'What total shall I put on your bill?'

'Add the inverted triangle to the total,' Papa says. 'He failed to observe the stop sign. We have witnesses.'

The little man pulls a face like a spoilt child.

'But I tell you she signalled me to proceed. She wanted me to.'

The leading lawyer gets up. His height intimidates everyone. Mother and Father plump out a bit, they sit down because they believe in justice, and they are quite calm.

'Your gabbling wears me out,' the lawyer says rudely.

Everyone jumps.

'I have a long career behind me,' the leading lawyer goes on, 'and considerable experience of the human heart. To sum up, I find you all guilty. You – ' he points to the little man – 'are condemned to see your own daughter disappear. That should teach you to let children under age make journeys without their parents' consent.'

'Please, your honour, I haven't got a daughter,' pleads the little man.

'It makes no difference,' the lawyer says. 'In that case it will be your wife. She can die of cancer, she's about the right age.'

The little man promptly begins to writhe with pain on the dusty floor.

'It's peritonitis,' he groans. 'Spare me, I implore you.'

Papa starts to snigger, and his black clothes immediately revert to being too big for him; he says:

'That isn't going to make you much richer, is it?'

And I wake up with a start.

I wait for an owl to skim on widespread silent wings above the eight neatly aligned beds in the green dormitory. Louisa is sucking her fingers.

Caroline hiccups happily in her sleep, and her arms flail wildly once or twice.

I get bored at night. I squat on my bed. In my white nightgown I am a bedouin watching for the dawn. If I shut my eyes I see the broad, flat horizon rising up to meet me; all of a sudden it tilts and I am falling. I fall through space, and the layers of atmosphere part one by one like torn membranes; right at the end there is a narrow passage circled in red, it contracts ever more narrowly and I can't, I cannot, enter it.

'Claire, Claire!'

She blazes towards me, she is a burn, she grabs me by the shoulders and I shoot out of my slippery skin, I land on my feet, arms wide, ready to bow like a circus acrobat.

'Well! Who'd have thought it!' Claire says, batting her eyelids in imitation of a long-lashed doll.

Each second she withdraws farther from me, and I follow her in a straight line which runs on for ever, where there is a wind which snatches your breath away. Claire goes too fast, I can't follow her, she pushes her hair back behind her ears, over her shoulder her eyes are laughing.

'Hurry and grow up, so I can tell you all about it.'

But she continues to withdraw from me. Her feet in pink mules fall over each other, yet she never trips.

'Listen, Claire, they're going to have a court hearing on you. They're all there, dressed in black . . .'

Claire does not take me seriously. Unfortunately she is still waiting for me to grow up.

She shuts herself up with Frédéric in the tomb like a little house. She slips her arm familiarly through his and says:

'I do hope you agree, darling, that the only place where

one really lives is the tomb. We'll have cushions every-where, and white flowers, and we'll suck in sunlight through a straw in the roof.

'If you go away, you'll only have to cover me lightly with earth, leaving my face free so that I can smile while I await your return. If I'm in a good mood, I'll even tuck my other smile into your breast-pocket so that a bit of it shows: my icy, bluish teeth, and my nose looking even smaller than it is, perhaps because my cheeks and chin have swollen. I ran into something, you know, as I was hurrying to meet you.

'One last point while I think of it: our rendezvous in the Pole Star is off. You see, the sky looks different from Peru, there's no Pole Star down there, my little sister looked it up in the atlas, and I wouldn't want you to go blundering round among stars we don't know. I should be afraid they might dig gaping black holes beneath your feet, disturbing our silence as they fill gradually with the deathlike murmur of deep waters.'

Something begins to howl in the darkness. The bier with the coffin upon it was set down. Charles's teeth started to chatter, and Mother held his jaw and hid his face against her skirt. The white roots have poked their way through the heaps of earth. And the ropes were paid out and it bumped against the sides of the hole, and everyone threw earth in upon it.

Everyone threw earth on it, Mama, I want Mama!

I want us to be children still, and I want it to be a Sunday in July, and I don't want us to sit down to lunch, I want Claire to come, and if it means I never grow up that's just too bad.

Sister Dolly switches on the lights, she comes with a funny hood over her shaven head, the girls are all standing round my bed, I see at once that Berthe is scared stiff because she has her mouth open. Sister Dolly makes me drink something bitter.

'It's only a bromide to soothe you. Now come along, dear, you've had a nasty nightmare but it's over now.'

But I know very well it will never be over.

'Never!' and I clutch her firm hand. 'You mustn't let me fall asleep, I'm too scared to go to sleep, I never want to go to sleep again.'

She promises to wake me up at once if I do, she will stay by me, the lights are put out, and one by one we drift back to sleep. Sister Dolly repeats 'The Lord is my shepherd'; she watches over us, and we are spotless lambs, protected.

When morning comes, Sister Dolly watches me while we brush our teeth, all eight of us standing in front of our eight washbasins, stark naked except for our slips.

'My goodness,' Caroline breathes, 'you never change yours.'

It's not my fault if Mother bought me seven all alike.

'You didn't half make a row in the night,' Caroline goes on.

She wants me to talk to her as before. I try, I say to her: 'It's your face that gives me nightmares, Berthe.'

I don't know what else to say. The big 245 h.p. Chevrolet drives on and crosses the mirror of the washbasin, distorted as if its bodywork were reflected in a shop-window. The square mountains of Peru file past, sometimes visible, sometimes hidden by dark glasses. I hope there are skyscrapers which never cease climbing into the clouds, streets drawn ruler-straight with yellow brushes. Big baboons, lounging nonchalantly in doorways, follow with their eyes silhouettes clad in low-necked yellow sweaters, black flared trousers, whispering as they pass:

'You there, walking and window-gazing on your own, you coming?'

No one answers. Claire has gone away. Mother totters down the corridor of our Paris apartment, the dark corridor which stretches out indefinitely – and Mother's figure shrinks, she staggers and puts both hands against the walls to keep her balance. With that slightly distraught look of helpless sorrow which she has acquired since Claire's death, she says:

'I'm looking for my little treasure.'

It's absolutely crazy. Papa has a napkin tied round his neck, his face goes red and so does his voice as he asks:

'What's this?'

Grandma's shoulders are bowed beneath her pearl necklaces; untiringly she hefts the weight of them in both hands, the same gesture endlessly repeated; she says:

'It's what keeps me young. That and my list of prohibitions, what more do you want?'

She is old enough to fall asleep on her feet. Valérie is lying face downwards, frozen on a photographic plate, her smile compressed between the sheets of glass. She feels there's nothing more to be said about Claire.

The white tiled surface of the shower-room dazzles dizzily, nothing restrains me any longer, I slide, pure speed, unhindered, on to the new white highway, around me the seconds fall like hail but I pass through them. In places they form a layer of thick ice like glass and I diverge, I enter into the warmth, the humid warmth that makes pointed spirals like worms, they penetrate the earth throwing up worm-casts behind them. When a tunnel appears I shall swim into it with my mouth open, to breathe in the earth's air and life.

I repeat after Claire: 'What's the sense? I can't understand. I don't understand anything. I no longer know what I'm waiting for. I no longer know where we stand.'

And then Sister Dolly claps her hands. Before taking our shower we have to line up, at arm's length from each other, for 'hands-on-hips', 'on-your-toes', 'knees-bend', one, two.

Immediately afterwards it is time for hot chocolate and rolls, you stuff your mouth full along with Caroline and you force yourself to laugh loudly so as to give the impression of sharing secrets which the other girls wouldn't be able to understand. On Wednesdays it's geometry, on Fridays we have a bath. When Sister Dolly has five minutes to herself she shuts herself up in the music-room and plays 'The Yellow Rose of Texas'. Always 'The Yellow Rose of Texas'.

Every morning we sit in the green classroom with arms folded, often the sun shines in on me, from behind Caroline bangs a book down on my head.

In December Caroline came running to look for me. I was reading *Moby Dick* on my bed in the green dormitory, while the rain poured down. I have been reading *Moby Dick* all the winter, I am beginning to believe that the white whale was really a black one, and that Captain Ahab is as much to blame as it is. What's the significance of their habit of everlastingly seeking each other out, on all the oceans?

'Berthe,' said Caroline, holding her breath with both hands under her navy-blue overall, 'there's a man waiting for you. A real man, I swear it, he's busy chatting up Sister Dolly, hurry up!'

I got off the bed and I forced myself to count to fifteen before condescending to make another move.

'Hurry!' Caroline said again.

Full of impatience, she herself pulled off my socks, she took off my overall, she undid the top button of my regulation dress, and she said:

'To make you look grown-up. Suppose it's Frédéric? You will tell me, won't you, Berthe?'

'Yes, Berthe.'

And only my lips moved.

In the vestibule which leads to the parlour I saw the back of a very tall, fair man in a pearl-grey flannel suit, like Papa's in the days when he was a real gay dog with a silver-mounted cane.

'Hup!' He turned round, snapping his fingers. 'Come along, then. Are you paralysed?'

I recognized Alain. I went forward to kiss him politely; he interrupted me, holding me at arm's length.

'But you're growing taller every day! And your hair! Are you letting it get long?'

'Like Claire. Aren't Mother and Father here?'

'I've come as deputy. And there was I thinking you'd be pleased about it!'

There were laughter-lines on his face. He took me by the shoulders, he forgot to let me go through the door first and he led me out to his car because there were too many people in the parlour. We settled ourselves with me behind the steering-wheel and him in the passenger's seat, shut in behind the windows streaming with rain. He took a white package at the end of a ribbon from the back seat.

'Guess what it is!'

'Cakes.'

Alain smiled. And then he tried further smiles, making the muscles of his jaw stand out when one of them went on too long. And then he folded his arms and said it was a bit cold in the car. He sighed. He folded his arms again. He suggested I should eat the cakes and we'd talk afterwards. He opened the box: chocolate éclairs – my favourites – and I began to munch them, making a noise on purpose. At first there wasn't any other sound. Except the rain and a light wind in the poplars.

Alain observed that the wind was rising. It wasn't true. He yawned, he gave me a tap on the knee.

'You haven't any curiosity. Aren't you going to ask me what I have to tell you?'

I had my mouth full. I half nodded, half shook my head.

When I had finished the five chocolate éclairs I put my hands on the steering-wheel and pretended to drive, listening to the rain's silence, except perhaps for the minute trembling of the cog-wheels inside Alain's wristwatch.

Alain lit a cigarette. He drew on it once or twice, he breathed deeply, he said:

'Well, I hope you'll be pleased: I'm going to marry Valérie.'

I lowered the window on my side, I stuck my head out and turned my face up and I felt the small cool drops run over my temples, down my nose and cheeks; I licked them up as they passed.

'I love rain.'

And I began to smile. This cool rain was falling on the whole world, on Peru, on Alaska, on Australia, spread over us like a coverlet, with the folds gently lapping days and nights, everything which leads up to the final blow, the one which gives you icy, bluish teeth and eyelids not properly closed. Alain was observing the effect of his surprise with shining eyes.

'Well, what do you say about it?'

He lifted my chin with his finger, and then he whispered with a little laugh:

'You know, if you had been older, I might have married you.'

Caroline was watching for me at the door, sitting on the plush sofa in the vestibule; with her eyes screwed up, she was making a face as if curiosity were causing the tip of her nose to itch. Girls went past slowly, in pairs, whispering the news they had received in the parlour. Soon it would be time to wash our hands for dinner. From the music-room came the sound of a piano playing 'The Yellow Rose of Texas'. Sister Dolly always plays 'The Yellow Rose of Texas'.

When I came in, Caroline rushed up to me, she thrust her mouth into my hair:

'Come on, Berthe, tell!'

I shrugged away from her.

'Nothing interesting, Berthe. Another man wanting to marry me. That's all.'